Robert Tyas

The language of flowers

Floral emblems of thoughts, feelings and sentiments

Robert Tyas

The language of flowers
Floral emblems of thoughts, feelings and sentiments

ISBN/EAN: 9783337271244

Printed in Europe, USA, Canada, Australia, Japan

Cover: Foto ©Andreas Hilbeck / pixelio.de

More available books at **www.hansebooks.com**

THE

LANGUAGE OF FLOWERS;

OR,

FLORAL EMBLEMS

OF

THOUGHTS, FEELINGS, AND SENTIMENTS.

" How oft doth an emblem-bud silently tell
What language could never speak half so well !"
Romance of Nature.

BY

ROBERT TYAS, M.A., LL.D., F.R.B.S.,

AUTHOR OF "FAVOURITE FIELD FLOWERS;" "FLOWERS FROM THE HOLY LAND," ETC.

With Twelve Coloured Groups of Flowers.

LONDON:
GEORGE ROUTLEDGE AND SONS,
THE BROADWAY, LUDGATE.
NEW YORK: 416, BROOME STREET.
1869.

INTRODUCTORY PREFACE.

BEFORE the different languages which are now common among men were developed, various animate and inanimate objects were made use of instead of words, for the purpose of giving expression to thoughts. Animals, birds, and flowers were emblems of individuals and their characteristics; and though sometimes erroneously assigned, they are yet very generally adopted.

Lions and foxes, eagles and hawks, and an almost endless number of quadrupeds and fowls of the air, have been thus applied and are still; yet, since most of us are little familiar with beasts and birds of prey, in these days of high civilization, it is natural that we should make choice of objects which are mixed up with our daily life, when we desire to give expression to our opinions or feelings by means of symbols rather than words.

In the vegetable kingdom we find objects most suitable for this purpose. We live in the midst of trees, and flowering plants and shrubs. We are daily surrounded by the denizens of the conservatory, the favourites of the flower-garden, or the native beauties of our fields. Many of these are associated in our minds with seasons of joy and sorrow, of pleasure and pain. Many of us have, laid up in some hidden spot, dried specimens of one flower or another, which was gathered by, or presented to us at a time of unusual happiness, or on an occasion of intense grief. These dried specimens are now and then looked upon, and they take us back into the past, and they help us in a remarkable degree to revive all the little incidents, pleasant or painful, connected with the time when we first became possessed of them.

Associations such as these give a charm to the Language of Flowers, and have tended to make it popular—in short, to render it universal in its adoption. It is, indeed, of no modern origin. It existed long before the oft-lamented days of chivalry, when faithful and reverential affection for the comparatively secluded lady could hardly be made known in any other way than by emblems, which were, it may be, of ambiguous import. Antique books are full of emblems formed by the grouping of flowers. From an ancient Romance we learn that a wreath of Roses was quite a treasure for lovers; and we read that a fair prisoner, Oriana by name, not having the opportunity of speaking or writing to her lover, informed him of her captivity by throwing to him from a lofty tower a Rose bathed in her tears. It is asserted that the Chinese possess an alphabet made up of figures of plants and roots. The rocks of Egypt are marked with representations of vegetables foreign to that country, which tell us of the conquests achieved by its ancient inhabitants.

The Language of Flowers is indeed as old as the hills; yet it never can become old, for every Spring reproduces its characters anew. We have a succession, year by year, of those emblems which, sufficiently distinct in the expression of our thoughts and feelings, are still characterised by a degree of ambiguity, which renders them singularly well suited to our use, at that particular period of life when our thoughts and our feelings are more commonly marked by changeableness and uncertainty; when the word uttered one moment is often regretted the next; when the polite attention which an admiring and impulsive youth pays to an attractive fair one, in the excitement of a pleasure party, is not unfrequently productive to him of regret and self-reproach; when a tender-hearted girl, having apparently encouraged the attentions of an intelligent but fortuneless youth, is annoyed at the recollection of her weakness. The innocent and pure sensations which induce that mutual regard between the opposite sexes in their youthfulness, are indeed well expressed by flowers. The mischievous little god, who is supposed to amuse himself by inflicting painful wounds on the youthful heart, is ever represented with wings, as emblematical of his fleeting and inconstant character, and with a fillet over his eyes, as indicating the uncertainty with which he aims his darts; as also symbolical of that blindness with which all mankind are proverbially said to be stricken, when they yield, without submitting to the guidance of reason, to the influence of his fatal inspiration. It is also the characteristic of such an inspiration to despise love bestowed ere sought for, and to account it worthless. It looks for difficulty in conquest, regarding the fair one who will not easily be won as only worth the winning.

In such a contest for victory, a half-avowal of reciprocal affection is more charming than an absolute acknowledgment; and the yielding up of a flower or a bouquet has made one far happier than the far-fetched expressions of a most tender note. The art of love-making is, with women, the art of self-defence; the more scrupulous and delicate they are, the more worthy are they of the homage rendered to them. Madame de Maintenon, who is said to have subdued the most inconstant of kings, revealed the secret of her power, when she said, "I never send him away content, never without hope."

Genuine affection knows neither trickery nor calculation. Simplicity and sincerity are its strength. That alone paves the way for a holy union, for a happy marriage. Without it all would languish and perish. A heart filled with indifference has never known what exalted devotion is. It is ignorant of those enchanting delicacies of feeling which impart value to a sigh, which render a look of importance, which give meaning to a word but half uttered, which stamp worth upon a flower that the one detains and the other allows to be taken. A heart filled with indifference is as far removed from happiness as from excellence. It is necessary to have known what love is; to have undergone some conflict in order to be good, tender, and generous. But it is not in the heart of cities,—it is in the fields, in the midst of flowers, that the affections flourish in purity and power.

The Language of Flowers lends its charms to friendship, to gratitude, to filial and maternal affection. Even the unfortunate may obtain help from this gentle language. The unhappy Roucher, alone in his prison, consoled himself by studying the flowers which his daughter used to gather for him; and, alas! a few days before his death, he sent to her two dried lilies, to express at the same time the purity of his soul and the fate that awaited him. How often may we see, in the crowded thoroughfares of our cities, children seeking to help their poor mothers, by offering small bouquets for sale! It was while presenting a Rose to his master, that the poet Sadi undertook to break his fetters: "Do well," he said, "to thy servant whilst thou hast it in thy power, for the duration of power is often as short as the blooming of this lovely Rose."

We have received from the ancients, and from Eastern

peoples, the greater part of the sentiments and emblems contained in this volume. In searching out the reason for assigning certain sentiments to particular flowers, we have generally found that time, instead of disproving their fitness, has rather given force to the symbolical character of the flower, and has confirmed the propriety of the application. Little study is needed in the science here taught.

The first rule in the Language of Flowers is, that a flower, presented in an upright position, expresses a thought; and to express the opposite of that thought, it suffices to let the flower hang down reversed. Thus, for example, a Rose-bud, with its thorns and leaves, says, "I fear, but I hope." If we present this same Rose-bud, reversed, it means "You must neither fear nor hope."

But there are divers modifications of a sentiment. It is easy to make these modifications even by means of a single flower. Take the Rose-bud, which has already served for an example. Stripped of its thorns, it says, "There is everything to hope for." Stripped of its leaves, it says, "There is everything to fear." One may also vary the expression of any flower, by altering its position. The Marigold, for instance: placed upon the head, it signifies, *sorrows of the mind;* placed above the heart, it speaks of *the pangs of love;* resting upon the breast, it expresses *ennui.* It must also be remembered that the pronoun of the first person is indicated by inclining the flower to the right; the pronoun of the second person by inclining the flower to the left. Such are the primary elements of our mysterious language. Friendship and affection should join in improving it. These sentiments, the most agreeable and most cherished in Nature, can alone bring to perfection that which they only have invented.

LIST OF PLATES.

———

xiii

ERRATUM.

In Plate V.,—Blue Bottle—Dog Rose—Garden Anemone, the word *Anemone* should be *Wallflower*.

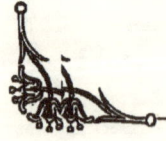

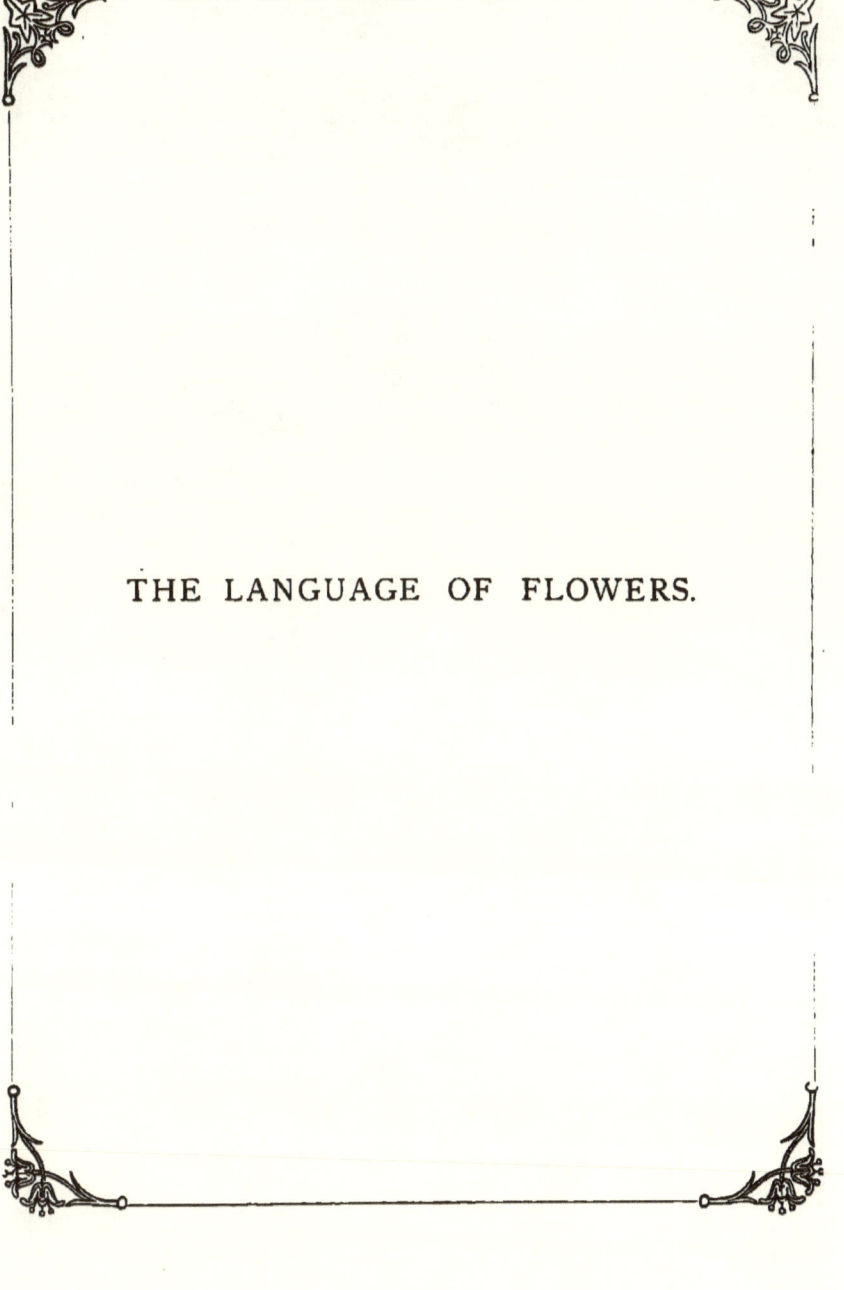

THE LANGUAGE OF FLOWERS.

LANGUAGE OF FLOWERS.

THE ACACIA (*Robinia Pseudacacia*).—PLATONIC LOVE.

> " It is a gentle and affectionate thought
> That, in immeasurable heights above us,
> At our first birth the wreath of love was woven,
> With sparkling stars for flowers."—COLERIDGE.

> " Love, the last best gift of heaven ;
> Love, gentle, holy, pure."—KEBLE.

THAT holy and pure affection, of which a flowering branchlet
of the Acacia is emblematical, has surely a heavenly original.
Beauty attracts ; but if unaccompanied by those endowments
of mind and heart which are truly worthy of esteem, it fails to
exercise a lasting power over any who are seeking for them,
and who possess the discernment which marks their absence ;
on the other hand, where genuineness of character exists, where
amiability, considerateness, and purity of heart and mind are
found,—though the casket which contains them may be of the
plainest, and repulsive rather than attractive,—the influence of

Acanthus as an ornament of the bower of our first parents in the garden of Eden, for he says:—

> "The roof
> Of thickest covert was inwoven shade,
> Laurel and myrtle, and what higher grew,
> Of firm and fragrant leaf; on either side
> Acanthus, and each odorous bushy shrub,
> Fenced up the verdant wall."

The motto of Callimachus, if he ever adopted one, must have been with reference to his art, "Excelsior," for he never satisfied his own ideal by the work he produced, but was ever aspiring after something of greater elegance and beauty than that which he had achieved.

The Acanthus delights in a hot climate, and to grow on the banks of large rivers. From a French writer we learn that it is found on the shores of the Nile; "le Nil du vert Acanthe admire le feuillage;" yet it thrives well with us. Pliny says that it is wonderfully well suited for a border plant and an ornament of our lawns. Chasers and carvers among the ancients, whose taste is very remarkable, decorated furniture, vases, and the most valuable dresses, with designs suggested by the foliage of the Acanthus. The poet Virgil speaks of the robe of the fair but frail Helen as being bordered with a garland of Acanthus wrought in relief; and when he wishes to praise works of art of much value, it is the Acanthus with which they are decorated,

> "Alcimedon duo pocula fecit,
> Et molli circum est ansas amplexus Acantho;"

4

spreading its light shade over our groves, enlivening them with the fresh greenness of its fine pinnated leaves, and beautifying them with its white pendulous and odoriferous flowers.

THE ACANTHUS (*A. mollis*).—THE ARTS.

IT is related of Callimachus, a famous statuary and archi-tect, but of unknown country, that, passing by the grave of a young lady, he drew near to scatter a few flowers upon her resting-place. The young lady had died some twelve months before. She was on the point of being married, and the intended union promised much happiness, of the enjoy-ment of which she was thus deprived. Callimachus' com-miseration prompted him to pay a tribute of regret, but he found that his offering had been already anticipated. The deceased young lady's nurse, collecting the flowers and the veil wherewith her mistress was to be adorned on her wedding day, put them together in a small basket. This basket she placed near the grave upon an Acanthus plant, and covered it with a large tile. In the following spring, the leaves of the Acanthus grew round the basket, but they, being checked by the edges of the tile, were forced round and grew towards its extremities. Callimachus, struck with the beauty of this rustic decoration, which appeared as though produced by the Graces in tears, conceived the design which has ever since adorned the capital of the Corinthian column. This possibly suggested to our immortal Milton the introduction of the

B 2

says it is thought that the name of Agrimony was given to this plant on account of the resemblance of its inverted flower-cups to the little hand-bells of the hermit. "For myself," she adds, "I think that Gratitude has accorded the name of the 'Country Nun' (*Religieuse des Champs*) to this pretty campanula, in honour of some kind, gentle, and obliging hospitaller, whose allotted duty it was to care for the sick, the poor, and the stranger."

Agrimony was formerly deemed a valuable tonic. It is still retained in our Materia Medica, but is seldom made use of. The herbalist counts it even now amongst his treasures, and they who prefer an infusion of herbs to plain water or fermented drinks, reckon Agrimony tea a refreshing beverage. It is by no means unpleasant to the palate, and the cause of temperance might be greatly promoted by its more general use, which would give it an additional claim to be regarded as the emblem of Gratitude.

THE COMMON ALMOND (*Amygdalus communis*).
THOUGHTLESSNESS.

> "The hope, in dreams, of a happier hour
> That alights on misery's brow,
> Springs out of the silvery almond flower,
> That blooms on a leafless bough."
>
> *Lalla Rookh.*

MYTHOLOGY hands down to us a fabulous account of the origin of the Almond-tree. It is sufficiently romantic to claim the character of a touching story. Among those who

6

and these bowls were made of beech, a wood which suits the craft of the turner, and affords great facilities to the carver.

This elegant model for the artist has become the emblem of the Arts. It may also be regarded as the emblem of genius, for if any obstacle opposes the growth of the Acanthus, we see that it yields, and, turning aside its forces, vegetates anew with fresh vigour ; so genius raises itself and grows by the very difficulties which it cannot subdue. It seems to say, as if in the very words of a remarkable bishop of one of our antipodean dioceses, " I do not know what failure means."

AGRIMONY (*Agrimonia Eupatoria*).—GRATITUDE.

PERHAPS nothing is more uncertain than the orthography of names of plants in colloquial language, especially in the transposition of the letter *r*. The name *argemon* (ἄργεμον) was assigned by Greek physicians to a plant supposed to be a cure for a *single white* speck on the cornea and sclerotic coat of the eye ; and botanists regard this as the same plant, or its best representative. By placing the *r* after the *g* we have the modern name, and it would appear that some etymologist among our continental neighbours supposed the word to be equivalent to the "Country Nun," whence its common name in France is, *Religieuse des Champs*.

The flowers of the Agrimony are campanulate, of a delicate yellow hue, suspended from the stalk like so many little bells. A French authoress, Madame de Chasteney by name,

Phyllis ran to the sea-shore. Demophon came not; then hope fled from her breast, she fell a prey to grief and died, some say by her own hand. She was transformed into an Almond-tree. Demophon had been detained, but was not faithless. Three months after, he returned; returned with heart desolated by the death of his betrothed. He offered sacrifices with all due rites, to appease the manes of the loved one; and the fable tells us that she was sensible of his return, for the Almond-tree which enclosed her in its bark, was suddenly covered with flowers, as if thus she would make known to him that death itself had not altered her affection.

This, the sweet Almond, and its variety, the bitter Almond, are extensively planted in the front of shrubberies and suburban gardens, where, on the first approach of spring, the branches, yet nude of foliage, are covered with the lovely flowers of this beautiful tree. Hence the fruit-germs are formed so early, that the later frosts destroy them, and they do not come to maturity. How meet an emblem of that thoughtlessness which too often leads youth to rash deeds, which mar their future prospects, and render the efforts of a lifetime nearly fruitless, when compared with the results which might, and probably would have followed, upon a thoughtful and deliberate course of action!

The spring frosts destroy the fruit in embryo; but instead of causing the flowers to fade and perish, they seem to endue them with fresh lustre,—

> " The almond-bloom doth show,
> When fully spread upon the leafless tree,
> A whiteness like the drifted snow;"

accompanied the Greeks to the siege of Troy, was Demophon, or Acamas, a son of Theseus and Phædra. Æthra, the mother of Theseus, was made captive by Castor and Pollux, when they rescued their sister Helen. She was taken to Sparta, and went with Helen when carried off by Paris, and was in constant attendance upon her. When Helen was summoned to

> see the wondrous deeds
> Of horse-taming Trojans and brass-coated Greeks,—*Il.* b. iii. l. 130.

on Paris and Menelaus having undertaken to decide the fate of Helen and of Troy by single combat,

> From her room she hastened, shedding tender tears;
> Not alone, but two handmaids with her followed,
> Æthra, Pittheus' child, and full-eyed Clymene ;—
> *Il.* b. iii. l. 142.

who (Æthra) was afterwards set free from slavery by the efforts of her grandson, Demophon.

Demophon on his return from Troy was shipwrecked on the coast of Thrace, where he met with Phyllis, daughter of the Thracian king, Sithon. A mutual attachment sprang up between Demophon and Phyllis and they became espoused, but ere the nuptials were celebrated, Demophon was summoned to Attica on the death of his father. Hope for a speedy return, and fear of a prolonged absence, led the young pair to fix too early a date for their reunion. The gentle Phyllis, with all the anxiety attendant on inactive waiting, counted the minutes which must elapse before the day, long looked for, would dawn ; it dawned at length, and nine times

7

tigers and lions delight to breathe. While we admire these flowers which adorn a climate so noxious to our constitutions, we ought to be thankful that our lot has fallen in more pleasant places. Here friendly Nature raises over our heads, on every side, verdant bowers; here she spreads under our feet a green carpet of grass, variegated by the purple crocus, the violet, the pretty daisy with its golden disk and white and rosy petals, and other pleasing products of Flora's domain.

The Aloe is used medicinally; the coarser kinds for domestic animals, the finer sorts for hepatic affections in the human species. It is intensely bitter. The roots, by which it is kept fixed in position, are very slender. Some of the more curious seem to derive nourishment chiefly from the atmosphere, and these present to us singular and bizarre figures.

Since disappointments, adversities and calamities, produce grief and bitterness of feeling, and thus tend to alienate our affections from surrounding objects; and, if they produce their best effect, lead us to seek comfort and support of a permanent character from the highest sources; so the bitter savour of the Aloe and its slight attachment to the earth, have suggested that it may fitly represent Bitterness and Grief in floral language.

THE AMARANTH.—Immortality, Unfading.

Some of the species of this order are ornamental, but the greater number are unattractive in appearance. They are prized because they seem to be the parting gift of autumn, and thus, pale and blanched at eventide, may be seen a group of profusely blooming trees. On the ensuing morning, as if refreshed by the freezing air of night, the bloom appears in rich rosy garb, and retains this new adornment,—though it may be in fact the decoration of death,—for a month or more, and it falls only when the trees are fully clad with leafy verdure.

THE ALOE.—Bitterness, Grief.

De Vaillant found very many species of the Aloe in the deserts of Namaquois. Some of these had leaves six feet long, closely packed and armed with a long spine; from the midst of the leaves there rises a stem to the height of a tree, adorned with flowers throughout. Others grow like the Cactus, bristling with spines; while some, again, are spotted, and have the appearance of serpents creeping upon the earth. Brydone says that the city of Syracuse was, as it were, covered with large Aloes in bloom; their beautiful and elegant stems giving to the headland above the beach the semblance of an enchanted woodland.

The Aloe is an extensive genus of exotics, comprising trees, shrubs, and herbaceous plants. The collection at the Museum de Paris is said to be the finest in the world. The Aloe thrives well with us, but chiefly, if not entirely, as a denizen of the greenhouse. These magnificent, not to say monstrous, members of the vegetable kingdom, are for the most part natives of barbarous Africa. There they flourish among rocks, in arid sands, in the glowing atmosphere which few lines. The author regrets the rapid flight of time and the fleeting beauty of summer flowers, and then adds,—

> "Je t'aperçois, belle et noble Amarante !
> Tu viens m'offrir, pour charmer mes douleurs.
> De ton velours la richesse éclatante ;
> Ainsi la main de l'amitié constante,
> Quand tout nous fuit, vient essuyer nos pleurs.
> Ton doux aspect de ma lyre plaintive
> A ranimé les accords languissants.
> Dernier tribut de Flore fugitive,
> Elle nous lègue, avec la fleur tardive,
> Le souvenir de ses premiers présents."

Queen Christina of Sweden, who wished to win for herself a name, by abdicating the throne that she might devote herself to literature and philosophy, founded an Order of Knights of the Amaranth. The decoration of this order is a gold medal, embellished with an Amaranth in enamel, with the motto, *Dolce nella memoria.*

In the floral games at Toulouse, the prize for the best lyric songs is a golden Amaranth.

Our own Milton was not unmindful of the claims of the Amaranth to be inwoven in his undying verse, though he imagines a flower which, transplanted from earth, should bloom for ever in heaven. Describing the worship of the Almighty Creator, when He had spoken to the angels of the "new heaven and earth," he says,

> "To the ground
> With solemn adoration down they cast
> Their crowns inwove with Amarant and gold,
> Immortal Amarant, a flower which once

and their flowers retain the brightness of their colour when dried. This property has gained for them the name Amarantos (ὁ ἀμάραντος), unfading, or the never-fading flower, which Pliny says is of a purple colour, velvety, and, though gathered, keeps its beauty while all others fade, and recovers its lustre if sprinkled with water.

The ancients were accustomed to make use of this flower in their religious ceremonies, and to deck their images with it. Poets have sometimes combined its lustre with the gloom of the cypress, as though they would intimate that their great sorrow for the dead was allied with enduring remembrances.

Malherbe, a French poet, who lived 1555—1628, assuming that his own fame was allied to that of his hero, says to Henri Quatre :—

> " Ta louange dans mes vers, d'Amarante couronnée,
> N'aura sa fin terminée qu'en celle de l'univers."

Love and friendship are also adorned with Amaranth. In the "Guirlande de Julie," the following lines claim the Amaranth as the appropriate flower wherewith to crown the gods :—

> " Je suis la fleur d'amour qu'Amarante appelle
> Et qui viens de Julie adorer les beaux yeux.
> Roses, retirez-vous, j'ai le nom d'immortelle,
> Il n'appartient qu'à moi de couronner les dieux."

In a pleasant idyl, Constant Dubos has sung so sweetly of this flower, regarding it as in some measure consoling us for the severity of winter, that we cannot refrain from quoting a loss to the floriculturist. The most haughty is the Guernsey Lily, a flower of charming beauty, resembling in its bearing and magnitude the Tuberous Polianthus, commonly known as the Tuberose. The Guernsey Lily is of a rich cherry-red colour, and, when lighted up by the direct rays of the sun, appears to be sprinkled, or to use an heraldic term, semée, with golden spots. The name of these lovely flowers is derived from the Greek verb *amarussein* (ἀμαρύσσειν), to sparkle or dazzle, which is very characteristic of their brilliant appearance.

The dazzling splendour of the Amaryllis when in full bloom, has sometimes a parallel in society, where a haughty belle in the grandeur of her prime beauty, set off by the skill of a fashionable *modiste*, eclipses the quiet attractions of as fair but more retiring sister, which are often destined to outlast those of her proud and disdainful rival, thus,—

" When Amaryllis fair doth show the richness of her fiery glow,
    The modest lily hides her head ; the former seems so proudly spread
    To win the gaze of human eye, which soonest brightest things doth spy.
    Yet vainly is the honour won, since hastily her course is run ;
    She blossoms, blooms,—she fades,—she dies,—they who admired, now
        despise."—*Flowers and Heraldry.*

THE AMERICAN COWSLIP (*Dodecatheon Meadia*).—
YOU ARE MY ANGEL.

DODECATHEON, a Greek word meaning *twelve gods*, is the name of a plant mentioned by Pliny, to whom the native habitat (Virginia) of this was certainly unknown. It is a

14

In Paradise, fast by the tree of life,
Began to bloom ; but soon for man's offence
To Heaven removed, where first it grew, there grows,
And flowers aloft, shading the fount of life,
And where the river of bliss through midst of Heaven
Rolls o'er Elysian flowers her amber stream ;
With these, that never fade, the spirits elect
Bind their resplendent locks enwreathed with beams,
Now in loose garlands thick thrown off ; the bright
Pavement, that like a sea of jasper shone,
Empurpled with celestial roses, smiled."

Moore introduces our flower in Lalla Rookh :—

" Amaranths, such as crown the maids
That wander through Zamara's shades."

This Zamara being said to be an ancient name for Sumatra.
The people of Batta, in that country, we are informed, when
not occupied by war, indulge in idleness, and in an inactive
life, spending their days in playing on a sort of flute, and
crowning themselves with garlands, of which the chief com-
ponent are the flowers of the Globe Amaranth, one of their
indigenous plants.

THE AMARYLLIS.—PRIDE, HAUGHTINESS.

THE number of species in this genus, as well as some
kindred genera of the same natural order, is very considerable. Florists say that they are very haughty plants ;
for, notwithstanding the most assiduous care, they often fail
to yield the reward of flowers. This is doubtless a great

THE ASH (*Fraximus excelsior*).—GRANDEUR.

> The Ash, aspiring upwards, rears its head,
> As if still higher from its native bed
> It sought to grow until it reach the sky;
> Yet 'tis so tied to earth that it will die
> If but some roots be bared of soil, and cease
> To draw supplies which make the tree increase :
> Thus man to grandeur raised and high estate
> By public favour, will, if that abate,
> Sink down again, and then his name shall ne'er
> Be heard with aught of love, or hate, or fear.—MS.

WE are told in the Edda that the immortal gods hold their court beneath an Ash tree which,

> " Far stretching his umbrageous arms,"—COWPER.

covers with its branches the whole surface of the world. When that veritable Chronicle was written, therefore, we infer from this statement that the author's, and no doubt the popular belief was, that the earth is " as flat as a dish," an opinion not yet quite exploded in the part of the world where we live, even in this the nineteenth century ! The highest point of this marvellous tree is said to touch the heavens, and the ramification of its roots to extend to the depths of the lowest regions. From the roots issue two fountains : in one of these wisdom is hidden, and in the other we are bid to seek for the knowledge of future events.

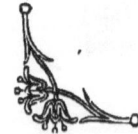
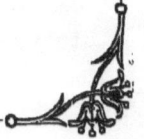

somewhat ostentatious appellation of an herb so small and unassuming as the American Cowslip, but extravagant admirers and botanists, even the great Linnæus, are not so very particular as to the fitness of names. This plant throws up one single stem, from the midst of a rosette of large leaves, which lie flat on the ground; on its summit are displayed, in the month of June, twelve inverted pretty light-purple flowers. It is highly ornamental. The stem dies off when the bloom is gone, and the root alone remains until the following season. It thrives best in shady situations and light loamy soils, but is not easily kept.

APPLE BLOSSOM.—PREFERENCE.

So much care has been bestowed upon the Apple tree to improve its fruit, on account of which it is very highly valued, that, whereas the Romans counted only twenty varieties, several hundreds are now reckoned in England and France. The tree has no beauty of form to make it attractive when grown as a standard; but in our orchards and fruit gardens, when the blossom is newly expanded, it is most ornamental and pleasing; and if our imagination passes on to a later season, anticipating the enjoyment of the fruit, the rich russets and other dessert kinds, which beautify our table and gratify our palate, we are much inclined to give to Apple Blossom the Preference over all other flowers, not excepting even the Rose, since that, when its beauty is fled, leaves us only an agreeable perfume to charm our sense of smell.

abounds with the white species. Persephone was wandering with her companions in the fields of Enna : there, in the meadow, sprung up a narcissus of marvellous beauty. Persephone saw it, longed to gather it, hastened away from her friends and put forth her hand to pluck the flower, when lo ! the earth opened, and Pluto seized the young goddess and bore her in his golden chariot to his palace in Hades, where he made her his mournful bride and queen of his domains. The Asphodel was dedicated to Persephone, as if in memory of her sad abduction, and by the ancients was much used in funeral ceremonies. The Shades, who have passed beyond the river Acheron, roam about over vast fields covered with this flower, and there they drink of the waters of the river of oblivion.

Longfellow, in a few verses called "The Two Angels," gives a curious conceit, wherein he combines the Asphodel and the Amaranth :—

"Two Angels, one of Life, and one of Death,
    Passed o'er the village as the morning broke ;
        *   *   *   *   *   *
And one was crowned with Amaranth, as with flame,
    And one with Asphodels, like flakes of light.
        *   *   *   *   *   *
And he who wore the crown of Asphodels,
    Descending at my door, began to knock;
And my soul sank within me——
        *   *   *   *   *   *
The door I opened to my heavenly guest,
    And listened——
        *   *   *   *   *   *

THE ASIATIC RANUNCULUS (*R. Asiaticus*).—YOUR CHARMS ARE RESPLENDENT.

THE "full Ranunculus of glowing red" is a native of the Levant, whence it was brought nearly three centuries ago. Though it is the common garden Ranunculus, and greatly admired when blooming, it is not so much cultivated as its beauty merits. The varieties of this species are innumerable, and are constantly increased by plants raised from seed, not any two seedlings producing flowers the same as the parent. This peculiarity may, perhaps, have caused it to be neglected by the professional florist. Varieties of established character and colour can be perpetuated and retained for a great number of years, by separating with a penknife all the buds in the crown of the tuber from each other, so that they will grow into independent plants. By these means the risk of losing the variety is greatly lessened. The flowers are brilliant in their tints, and may be enumerated as coffee-coloured, crimson, gray, olive, orange, purple, red, rosy, spotted, striped, yellow, white, &c. Scarcely any plant offers such variety in colour, or anything so striking to the eye.

THE ASPHODEL.—MY REGRETS FOLLOW YOU TO THE GRAVE.

THE Asphodel is an ornamental genus of plants of easy culture, and may be increased rapidly. It affords much nourishment to sheep in Apulia, where a large extent of land about the chalk quarries at Compton and Wanborough, as we learn from a paper on the "Flora of Godalming," kindly sent to us by the Author, J. D. Salmon, Esq., M.B.S. It may easily be overlooked in such rural places, for

> " The humble bee
> Seems sipping honey from the purple flower ;"—
> *Favourite Field Flowers.*

and we pass on, not thinking that we have just glanced upon so singular an effort of Nature in the vegetable kingdom. How often do we miss, in our journey through life, things of the greatest interest and most remarkable peculiarity, by prepossession of the mind with an object differing from the present unperceived reality !

BALM (*Melissa officinalis*).—PLEASANTRY.

THE generic name Melissa (Μέλισσα) was no doubt given to this because it is pre-eminently *a bee* plant, an especial favourite with that ever active and industrious insect. Its flowers abound in honey, as others in the Natural Order Labiatæ. Its fresh leaves have the agreeable flavour of lemon. This fragrance is evanescent and not to be perceived in the dried plant. It used to be thought much of as a strengthener of the nerves, and as giving relief to the hypochondriac. An infusion of its leaves is now valued as a pleasant and cheering tea in the heat of the summer.

Then with a smile that filled the house with light—
' My errand is not Death, but Life,' he said ;
And, ere I answered, passing out of sight,
    On his celestial embassy he sped.

'Twas at thy door, O friend, and not at mine,
    The angel with the Amaranthine wreath,
Pausing, descended; and, with voice divine,
    Whispered a word that had a sound of Death.

Then fell upon the house a sudden gloom—
    A shadow on those features fair and thin ;
And softly, from that hushed and darkened room,
    Two angels issued, where but one went in."

Does the writer wish to imply that the Asphodel typifies this present Life, a season of disappointments and regrets, while the Amaranth represents Death, as the period which grants to the prepared spirit an entrance into Life immortal ?

THE BEE OPHRYS (*O. apifera*).—ERROR.

" See, Delia, see this image bright ! why starts my fair one at the sight?
It mounts not on offensive wing, nor threats thy breast with angry sting ;
Admire, as close the insect lies, its thin-wrought plume and honey'd
    thighs,
Whilst on this flow'ret's velvet breast, it seems as though 'twere lull'd to
    rest,
Nor might its fairy wings unfold, enchain'd in aromatic gold :
Think not to set the captive free, 'tis but the picture of a bee."—SNOW.

THIS is one of the most remarkably beautiful of our indigenous orchids. Its ordinary habitat is in open meadows, by woodsides, on chalky soils. It is found, but sparingly,

The Yellow Balsam has been found at Fountain's Abbey, Yorkshire; in Westmoreland, and in Surrey, but rarely; it is an annual, blooming in the hot months of July and August. The flowers, and especially the capsules, merit close inspection. When ripe, the seed-vessels, if touched however lightly, instantaneously separate at the base and curl backward, jerking the seeds to a considerable distance, whence it has acquired the common name of Touch-me-not. Darwin thus notices this peculiarity :—

> " With fierce distracted eye Impatiens stands,
> Swells her pale cheeks and brandishes her hands;
> With rage and hate the astonished groves alarms,
> And hurls her infants from her frantic arms."

Impatience is a very common and ruinous folly. A writer in the popular serial, St. Paul's, says, "the greatest of all waste of time is hurry. Impatience is the robber of time; whereas procrastination, as we know by the copybooks, is a mild and gentle thing, whose petty larcenies are accompanied by no violence. Impatience is always rushing headlong into tangled and thorny thickets to explore some promising and picturesque short-cut to nowhere. Impatience is always on the point of finding a fool's paradise in a mare's nest. Impatience goes on from failure to failure, attempting to make silk purses out of sows' ears. Impatience keeps tossing over new acquaintances in a perpetually disappointed rapture of anticipation of ideal perfection; like some insane bee buzzing about in search of a flower which should be entirely constructed of white wax and clarified honey."

BALM OF GILEAD.—Cure. Healing.

THERE is a Fir-tree known as the Balm of Gilead, which exudes a gummy substance, the medicinal qualities of which, however, do not surpass those of common turpentine. There is very great doubt about the tree which yielded the inestimable balm so highly valued by the Jews. It is alleged by some writers that it does not now exist in Palestine. It was regarded as a panacea for "the thousand ills that flesh is heir to." We not unfrequently employ the word *balm* in a moral and figurative sense, when we mean anything which we deem likely to temper grief and soothe the afflicted. A benevolent disposition and sincere friendship are true balms, serving to heal the wounds of the mind, which are far more difficult to sustain with patience than physical evils.

BALSAM (*Impatiens Nolitangere*).—IMPATIENCE.

THE Yellow Balsam, though one of our native plants, is by no means common. It delights in shady woods, where moisture abounds. So it has been written of it:

" In the thick and deep recess of a blooming wilderness,
   Tangled weeds concealed from view—what alone by sound we knew—
   A bubbling murmuring stream, unlit by glittering beam
   Of the gorgeous sun above this delightful cool alcove.
   On the soft and moistened bank, which the brooklet's waters drank,
   'Mid the ravelled weeds there grew, pleasing to our searching view,
   Yellow Balsam's blossoms gay, scattered o'er in thick array,
   With the shining scarlet spots Nature to this flower allots."—

Favourite Field Flowers.

THE BEECH (*Fagus sylvatica*).—PROSPERITY.

EVERY school-boy must know the opening lines of the first Eclogue of Virgil's Bucolics, wherein Melibœus, seeing Tityrus lying at ease under a Beech-tree, thus accosts him :—

> " Tityre, tu patulæ recubans sub tegmine fagi
> Silvestrem tenui musam meditaris avena ; "

which is as if he had said in simple English, "O Tityrus, thou, reclining under the shade of a wide-spreading Beech-tree, rehearsest a sylvan song upon the slender pipe ;" apparently envying the rustic owner of the woolly flock he tends ; thinking how happy must be the man, who, prosperity favouring, can thus enjoy at will the very pure air of the open fields, shaded from the mid-day sun by the spreading foliage of the Beech-tree.

Not any other of our trees forms so ample a roof, and if you seek shelter from a pelting shower, or a shade from the scorching sun, you will find it best

> " Beneath the shade which Beechen boughs diffuse."

This marked feature in the Beech has seldom passed unnoticed by the poet who has named it in his verse. Gray, in his Elegy, combines it in the mind of village swains with the memory of some departed patriarch :—

> " There at the foot of yonder nodding Beech,
> That wreathes its old fantastic roots so high,
> His listless length at noontide would he stretch,
> And pore upon the brook that bubbles by."

24

BASIL (*Ocymum Basilicum*).—HATRED.

POVERTY has been represented as a female form covered with rags, seated near a Basil plant. It is also a common saying that Hatred has the eyes of a Basilisk, which, according to several ancient and learned authors, was the King of Serpents, wearing a royal crown upon its head, blighting herbage with its breath, and killing by a glance of its eye. Why Sweet Basil should be made the emblem of Hatred it is difficult to say. The French word *Basilic*, corresponding to our specific term *Basilicum*, is also applied to the fabulous reptile spoken of above. There may be some supposed resemblance to the fanciful pictures of the reptile in the labiate flower, which may have suggested the emblematic use; but the flower is not only not hurtful, but a culinary aromatic used by our continental neighbours. Moore, in Lalla Rookh, speaks of—

> " The Basil tuft, that waves
> Its fragrant blossom over graves ; "

and tells us that it is commonly found in churchyards in Persia, where it is called Rayhan ; perhaps some superstitious passer-by at dim twilight, full of dread fear of hobgoblins and shades of the departed, may have mistaken the flower for the reptile, and thought that the glaring eyes of this "*monstrum horrendum*" were threatening him with death and destruction.

farmer. On account of the keen acidity of the fruit, it is made the emblem of Tartness. We are also told that the flowers are endued with such extreme irritability, that at the lightest touch, all the stamens coil themselves around the pistil: hence they exhibit the characteristic sharpness of persons whose anger is instantaneously aroused by the most trivial causes.

THE BIRCH TREE (*Betula pendula.*)—GRACEFULNESS.

THIS species of the Birch is an exceedingly graceful tree. Coleridge speaks of it as

> "Most beautiful
> Of forest trees, the lady of the woods;"

a title which it fully deserves. Its spray is more slender than that of other species, and also larger. The foliage has an elegant pensile appearance, as the weeping willow, and like it is set in motion by the faintest breath of zephyr. In his poem, the "Isle of Palms," Wilson has observed this, and applied the epithet, "weeping," to our tree,—

> " On the green slope
> Of a romantic glade we sate us down,
> Amid the fragrance of the yellow broom,
> While o'er our heads the Weeping Birch-tree streamed
> Its branches, arching like a fountain shower."

The Birch is of rapid growth, and, at any age, one or two are a pleasing addition to small plantings in the vicinity of our dwellings.

The Beech, though perhaps neither so handsome nor so valuable as the oak, yet rivals it in appearance, and grows more rapidly, so rapidly indeed that on that account it might well claim to be the emblem of prosperity, while it deserves to be so regarded for its abundant mast, which in days of yore fattened deer and swine. Beech-nuts yield a sweet oil, which the French peasantry not unwillingly mingle with their diet.

THE BERBERRY (*Berberis vulgaris*).—TARTNESS. SHARPNESS.

THE Berberry is an ornament to our shrubberies, when adorned with its pendulous racemes of flowers in spring, or when its bunches of bright red berries are ripe in autumn. The green of the leaves, which are pleasantly acid, has a bluish or yellow tinge. The odour of the flowers is agreeable when somewhat diluted with air, but offensive to our olfactory nerves, if it comes in contact with them when just emitted from the bloom. The fruit is so sharply acid, that birds reject them. They are, nevertheless, valued as garnish, for which purpose they are pickled ; and they form an agreeable preserve, when boiled with sugar. The Poles extract a fine yellow dye for leather from the root-bark. The inner bark of the stem when applied to linen, with alum, will dye it yellow. It is asserted by many writers that the Berberry affords shelter and nourishment to an insect (*Æcidium Berberidis*), which produces rust in corn, so that it is a great foe to the

Pliny. Its habit is that of the vine, though it has no tendrils, hence in its upward tendencies it requires a firm support, by which it climbs to the height of some ten feet. In return for this it adds considerable beauty to the trees which grant their aid.

BLACK MULBERRY (*Morus nigra*).—I WILL NOT SURVIVE YOU.

ITALY is the birthplace of the Black Mulberry-tree, which is cultivated on account of the delicacy of its fruit. It is by no means a common tree; why, we know not, but it may be that, as with the Walnut, he who plants one never eats its fruit. The Mulberry certainly does not bear fruit for very many years, but afterwards its fruitfulness increases with its age, and the fruit is larger, and its flavour pleasanter. The Mulberry, like the Strawberry, does not undergo acetous fermentation in the stomach. It allays thirst, and is so refreshing in its effects that Horace's lines seem quite justified :—

> " He shall with vigour bear the summer's heat,
> Who, after dinner, shall be sure to eat
> His Mulberries, of blackest ripest dyes,
> And gathered ere the morning sun arise."—FRANCIS.

Ovid's story about Pyramus and Thisbe is well known: how that the latter was a lovely damsel of Babylon, and that Pyramus lived in the house adjoining. The pair became enamoured; but their attachment was not approved of by

BITTER-SWEET NIGHTSHADE (*Solanum Dulcamara*).
TRUTH.

TRUTH has been justly regarded as the mother of Virtue, the daughter of Time,—since time only in many cases brings truth to light,—and queen of the world, because in the end it must have full sway. The facts revealed when the truth is known may produce mental pain, and bitterness of heart, but these are accompanied by the gratification which it gives, and the relief from doubt and anxiety it affords. Such are the effects of the leaves of Bitter-Sweet Nightshade on the palate, when they are chewed; first a keen sensation of bitterness, followed immediately by sweetness. Beaumont and Fletcher characterise truth very appropriately :—

> "Truth, though it trouble some minds,
> Some wicked minds, that are both dark and dangerous,
> Preserves *itself:* comes off pure, innocent !
> And like the sun, though never so eclipsed,
> Must break in glory !"

The plant is described as a deciduous twiner; but alleged to renew its foliage twice yearly, as do our evergreens; it delights in dark and shady places, and thus resembles truth in her supposed characteristic of being pleased to abide at the bottom of wells.

BLACK BRYONY (*Tamus communis*).—BE MY SUPPORT.

THIS twining plant is common throughout Europe, bearing yellowish green flowers, and oblong fleshy berries, of a shining orange red. It is supposed to be the *Uva Taminia* of

BLACK POPLAR (*Populus nigra*).—COURAGE.

THE Black Poplar was consecrated to Hercules because he slew Cacus who stole part of the cattle which he brought into Italy. This feat the hero accomplished in a cave by Mount Aventine, where the Poplar was abundant. Virgil records this, speaking of Hercules under his name Alcides :—

> " Come, then, with us to great Alcides pray,
> And crown your heads, and solemnize the day.
> Invoke our common god with hymns divine,
> And from the goblet pour the generous wine,
> He said; and with the Poplar's sacred boughs,
> Like great Alcides, binds his hoary brows."

Hercules performed wondrous exploits and possessed extraordinary courage. It is alleged that in his courageous descent into the lower world his head was covered with poplar, and that the outsides of the leaves were blackened by the fumes of the atmostphere. This tree may well then be made the emblem of his most prominent quality. The Black Poplar is a valuable tree ; grows rapidly ; delights in moist localities ; its light bark supplies fishermen with floats ; its timber suits the turner and the patten-maker, and supplies capital flooring-boards ; it does not readily catch fire, and, in short, it is a most serviceable tree for a variety of purposes. Even thus courage is of great use, not only in the battle field of armies, but in the battle of life, where ever-varying circumstances are continually demanding the exercise of this inestimable quality.

their respective parents. They found means to arrange a meeting at the tomb of Ninus. Thisbe first came to the place of rendezvous, where she saw a lion which had torn an ox in pieces just before, and she fled alarmed, losing in her flight her garment, which the wild animal soiled with blood. Pyramus, finding her garment covered with blood, supposed she had been murdered, and in his frenzy destroyed himself beneath a Mulberry-tree. Thisbe ventured to return, when she found her lover dead, and killed herself in her grief. Their mingled blood was drunk up by the tree, the fruit of which was thenceforth black :—

> " Dark in the rising tide the berries grew,
> And white no longer, took a sable hue ;
> But brighter crimson springing from the root,
> Shot through the black, and purpled all the fruit."

Cowley alludes to the fable in speaking of this tree :—

> " In two short months her purple fruit appears,
> And of two lovers slain the tincture wears."

A French author commends the maiden's modesty in her dying moments :—

> " Elle tombe, et, tombant, range ses vêtements ;
> Dernier trait de pudeur, même aux derniers moments.
> Les nymphes d'alentour lui donnèrent des larmes ;
> Et du sang des amants teignirent, par des charmes,
> Le fruit d'un mûrier proche, et blanc jusqu'à ce jour,
> Éternel monument d'un si parfait amour."

THE BLUE BOTTLE (*Centaurea Cyanus*).—DELICACY.

THIS species of the Centaurea is so ornamental, its flower being of the intense blue of a cloudless sky, that it is often introduced into the garden. Under cultivation the flowers become larger, and the colour varies. It is one of the prettiest of Flora's gems among ripening grain. Its specific name Cyanus immortalizes a youth, whose time was spent in making wreaths of such flowers as were in bloom, through his great love for them. This flower he specially admired, and his chief ambition was to clothe himself in garments of the same celestial hue. Being found dead, lying amid Blue Bottles which he had collected in the field, Flora transformed him into the Centaurea Cyanus, as a graceful acknowledgment of his veneration for her. It has been, therefore, made the emblem of that delicacy which marks the devotion of an inferior, feeding upon hope, the realization of which it does not look for.

THE BLADDER-NUT (*Staphylea pinnata*).—FRIVOLOUS AMUSEMENT.

A SHRUB of some pretension to beauty, and therefore found in our garden groves. The leaves are pinnate, which is a pleasing form, and render it graceful. The fruit grows in a bunch, as its generic name indicates. The nuts are very curious, and hang on the tree for a long time. These

BLACK-THORN (*Prunus spinosa*).—DIFFICULTY.

THIS bushy shrub is common enough in our hedgerows, where its white flowers display themselves to advantage in March and April, ere the Hawthorn is in bloom, though Burns says :—

> "The Hawthorn's budding in the glen,
> And milk-white is the sloe;"

as if both were flowering at the same time. The bark is of a brown hue nearly approaching black, and the branches terminate with a sharp thorn. The well-known fruit under the name of the sloe, is small, somewhat oval, of a blackish purple, and is covered with a fine whitish powdery bloom. The juice is very sour, astringent, but not disagreeable at the season of perfect ripeness. It is said to be largely used in making British Port wines; we hope its astringent properties are not applied to the improvement (?) of rough-flavoured wines of Portugal (so called.) The tree furnished the means to dishonest people of adulterating tea, by the admixture of its leaves with the products of China. A Parliamentary inquiry proved that it formed fictitious tea in England to the extent of four million pounds a year !

There is a proverbial saying made use of when a perplexing question comes before us, "It is a perfect bundle of thorns; we don't know where to begin, nor how to act!"

Botanists class this plant among the squills. Its specific name was fancifully given to it, from the absence of the letters, A I, A I, *woe! woe!* which are said to be inscribed on the petals of other hyacinths. Its delicious fragrance, and the rich beauty of its deep blue-purple bells, have apparently claimed for it a place in floral language as the emblem of kindness.

BORAGE (*Borago officinalis*).—BLUNTNESS. RUDENESS.

APULEIUS says that *Borago* is a corruption of *corago*, a name given to the plant because of its cordial properties. It formed an ingredient in the beverage called *cool tankard*, though it may be supposed to be rather warming than cooling from the old adage, " I, Borage, always bring courage." Dodonæus, as quoted by Gerarde, says, " Those of our times do use the flowers in salads, to exhilarate and make the minde glad. There be also many things made of them, used for the comfort of the *heart*, to drive away sorrow and increase the joy of the minde." Since men, who are civil and respectful when sober, often become blunt and rude in manner when under the influence of warming cordials, this warming property may have led to Borage being used as the emblem of Bluntness and Rudeness. It is, indeed, deemed a suitable representative of these characteristics, on account of its rough and shaggy appearance, the whole plant hanging loosely, and being covered with rough hairs. Yet its alleged good properties remind us that a brusque manner often marks a man of explode with a loud noise, when pressed between the fingers, and afford a trifling amusement to children. Now and then sedate adults vie with the juveniles in this explosive sport, for which its sentiment has been assigned, perhaps with a degree of contemptuousness which borders on ill-nature. Roman Catholics are said to string them for use as rosaries; and poor people on the Continent form necklaces of the seeds, which are highly polished.

THE BLUE BELL (*Scilla nonscripta*).—KINDNESS.

THIS pretty flower, commonly called the Wild Hyacinth, abounds in the spring months in our shady woods. Nowhere have we seen it so profusely blooming, as in the hazel copses around Godalming, a neighbourhood full of picturesque beauty, where, interspersed with the wood anemone, and a host of other flowers, it appears to great advantage. The French call it *Jacinthe des Bois*, on account of its fondness for woodland shades, a characteristic which Elliott, the Corn-law rhymer, has noticed in his vigorous verse :—

> " Shade-loving Hyacinth ! thou comest again,
> And thy rich odours seem to swell the flow
> Of the lark's song, the redbreast's lovely strain,
> And the stream's tune ;—best sung where wild flowers blow,
> And ever sweetest where the sweetest grow."

Keats, in his poem " Fancy," was mindful of its shade-loving character, and calls the Blue Bell the Queen of May,—

> " Shaded Hyacinth, alway sapphire Queen of the Mid-May."

verdure in the great heat of summer, as well as in the severe frosts of winter, and demands little care from the gardener for years, until, as in some soils, it grows too high and too thick to be pleasing. Then it needs to be taken up, sub-divided, and re-planted. It was much admired by the Romans, by whom the taller-growing kinds were cut into grotesque forms, to resemble men, animals, &c. It is a tree which appears to be unchanged by time; hence it well repre-sents that stoicism which, according to Zeno, distinguishes the wise man, who is not moved either by joy, grief, or any other passion, and who looks upon all events as ruled by inevitable necessity.

The wood of the Box-tree is highly valuable, especially in the estimation of the lover of knowledge, for the facility which it gives to artists to convey pictorial lessons in every branch of science, whereby the meaning of a writer is ren-dered more precise and exact to the reader; it is also useful for many other purposes, which are too numerous to mention here.

THE BRAMBLE (*Rubus fruticosus*).—ENVY.

THE Bramble is very well known to us, growing every-where in our woods and hedges. Its long trailing prickly stems throw themselves outwards from the hedges, by our road-sides and footpaths, and now and then lay hold of the loose parts of the garments of pedestrians, who cannot readily release themselves. On this account we have heard these kind heart and thorough sincerity. Such an one is greatly to be preferred to the man of polished manner, whose every word is honey, and every look a smile, but whose whole soul is bent upon making use of you solely for his own advantage. Borage is a great favourite with the honey-bee. We have sown the seeds extensively in some years, and valued it, not only because we saw our honey-gathering friends continually busied about its flowers, but for the beautiful blue colour of the large blossoms, which greatly ornamented our grounds.

A BOUQUET OF FLOWERS.—GALLANTRY.
POLITENESS.

THERE is opportunity for the display of great taste in the arrangement of a Bouquet of Flowers. The materials vary, of course, with the seasons of the year; but good taste and a proper appreciation of the character of the person to whom the bouquet is to be offered, will generally produce a satisfactory result. It is a mark of the politest attention, and shows an anxious desire to give gratification.

BOX (*Buxus sempervirens*).—STOICISM.

BOX is most commonly known as a very useful, durable, and pleasing evergreen edging to our flower-beds. Its exceeding slow growth renders it the more valuable for this purpose. It thrives well even under the drip of trees, maintains its

branches facetiously called "lawyers," in some parts of England, where these gentlemen are supposed not to let a client off easily when they get one.

The bramble creeps along through hedges, strikes roots afresh, keeps off sun and air from the young shoots of the hawthorn, and seems to choke every thing which it comes near; just as envy, stealthily, treacherously, and spitefully, seeks to destroy the character and possessions of one who is seemingly prosperous in wealth, or friends, or esteem. Miss Twamley assigns the bramble to a girl who is crabbed, and displeased with another more amiable than herself,—

> "Yon Bramble fling to Rachel Rann
> So crabby and so spiteful;"

and most aptly does this wild, rough, and prickly plant befit this very objectionable trait.

Yet the Bramble affords us some pleasure by its pretty pink flowers, and perhaps still more by its fruit, the blackberry, which, when fully ripe, are very agreeable to the palate, and cooling ; if eaten before, they are unpleasant and sour, and if when over ripe, they are nauseous. They make agreeable tarts, but are somewhat insipid.

A BROKEN STRAW.—Rupture. Dissension.

The custom of breaking a straw, to intimate the rupture of all mutual obligations, may be traced to a very early period. Madame de la Tour claims for it even a royal origin. She says that the old Chroniclers relate how Charles the Simple, in the year 922, when he saw that he was forsaken by the chief of his barons, summoned an assembly in the Champs de Mai, at Soissons. He looked among them for friends, but found only a factious crew, whose audacity his own weakness served only to increase. Some reproached him with indolence, with his prodigalities, and for his blind trust in Haganon, his minister. Others complained loudly of his dishonourable concessions to Raoul, the Norman chief. Surrounded by this seditious multitude, he entreated, he promised, and sought to escape them by betraying fresh weaknesses, but all in vain. When they saw him devoid of all moral courage, their insolence knew no bounds; they declared that he was no longer their king. At these words, which they uttered with every gesture of violence, and accompanied with threats, they advanced to the foot of the throne, broke some straws which they had in their hands, cast them rudely upon the ground and withdrew, having expressed by this meaning action that they renounced their allegiance to him.

This is the most ancient example of the kind known to us; but it proves that, long ago, this expressive mode of breaking treaties was in use, since the great vassals of the weak king did not consider that any words were needed in explanation; they felt sure that they would be understood, and they were so.

There is a considerable space of time between the above and the comic scene in the *Dépit amoureux* of Molière; yet the one is the origin of the other; at least they have their source in the same popular custom ; there is only the difference of time. That which of old served to dethrone a monarch, and revolutionize a nation, is now used only to express the desolation of a heart. Happy are the loving hearts whose discords terminate so well as the revolutions of early times ! Yet far happier they, where dissension never arises, though, it may be, they are few in number, since—

> " Alas—how light a cause may move
> Dissension between hearts that love !—
> Hearts that the world in vain had tried,
> And sorrow but more closely tied ;
> That stood the storm when waves were rough,—
>   *   *   *   *   *   *
> A something light as air,—a look,
>   A word unkind or wrongly taken—
> Oh! love, that tempests never shook,
>   A breath, a touch like this hath shaken.
>   *   *   *   *   *
> And hearts, so lately mingled, seem
> Like broken clouds,—or like the stream,
> That smiling left the mountain's brow,
>   As though its waters ne'er could sever,
> Yet, ere it reach the plain below,
>   Breaks into floods, that part for ever !"
>   MOORE, *Lalla Rookh.*

The Broom and its kindred genera were great favourites among the Greeks and Romans. One writer says that wherever Cytisus grows, there bees never abandoned their hives ; and Pliny says of him (Aristomachus), that he was so devotedly fond of bees, that for fifty-eight years of his life he continued to raise swarms. The Spanish Broom (*Spartium iunceum*), a yellow-flowered species, is cultivated for its beauty

39

and perfume when in bloom. It is grown for feeding sheep in France, and in Spain is much used for cordage. Scott notices the toughness of the fibrous roots, which would make them useful for such a purpose :—

> " And now, to issue from the glen,
> No pathway meets the wanderer's ken,
> Unless he climb, with footing nice,
> A far projecting precipice.
> The Broom's tough roots his ladder made ;
> The hazel's saplings lent their aid ;
> And thus an airy point he won."

An indigenous species (*S. scoparium*) is very beautiful in its native wilds, where the Broom bears her blossoms,

> " Yellow and bright as bullion unalloyed,"

in the pleasant months of April, May, and June, of which Wordsworth was thinking when he wrote,—

> " 'Twas that delightful season, when the Broom,
> Full-flowered, and visible on every steep,
> Along the copses runs in veins of gold."

In bushy places, thickets, and on sandy hills, it displays its beauties most charmingly ; and Burns admired it so greatly that it inspired him with the following exulting lines,—

> " Their groves o' sweet myrtle let foreign lands reckon,
> Where bright beaming summers exalt the perfume ;
> Far dearer to me yon lone glen o' green breckan,
> Wi' the burn stealing under the lang yellow Broom.

Far dearer to me are yon humble Broom bowers,
    Where the bluebell and gowan lurk lowly unseen ;
For there, lightly tripping amang the sweet flowers,
    A-listening the linnet, oft wanders my Jean."

According to Thompson's London Dispensatory, this species
is useful for a vast number of purposes in medicine.

BUCKBEAN (*Menyanthes trifoliata*).—CALMNESS. REPOSE.

THE Buckbean is one of our native plants, found frequently
in boggy places and marshes. The flowers are white, sometimes flesh-coloured, tipped outside with a rosy pink. From
the flower-cup, often white as alabaster, springs forth a tuft
of filaments of great delicacy and dazzling whiteness.   No
adequate notion of the elegance of this plant can be conveyed
in words. Those who have once seen it, lightly pendant
over the clear streamlet or the limpid water of its favourite
habitat, will never forget its appearance. The bright trans-
parency of the rivulet seems increased by the reflection of
this pretty dweller on its borders. The Buckbean is said
never to bloom in stormy weather, but only when the air
is calm and in repose : and this quiet calmness it appears
to impart to surrounding objects.

Not only is the Buckbean ornamental, but useful.   The
bee delights to sip its sweetness.   It is a medicinal herb ;
and in times past was beneficially used to allay fever, to
soothe rheumatic pains, and to reduce suffering in the joints.

41

For these purposes an infusion of its dried leaves was made, and a wine-glassful administered twice or thrice daily; therefore it seems fully to have merited its position as the emblem of calmness and repose which it yielded to the suffering.

BUGLOSS.—FALSEHOOD.

THIS plant, of different species, has been made the emblem of Falsehood, because of its use in many kinds of colouring substances. In very early times, *Anchusa tinctoria*, the Dyer's Bugloss, was made use of to colour the face before more delicate means were found out. This is, perhaps, the least hurtful, and possesses many advantages. It maintains its colour for some days, and water revives it as it revives natural colours; and it does not tarnish the skin.

> " But the blush which tinges the maiden's cheek,
> Whose heart is innocent, gentle and meek,"

how can it be imitated? Art, the most skilful, destroys it, never to be restored. Do we desire to please for a long time?—do we desire to please always? Then let us dismiss falsehood from our heart, from our tongue, and from our countenance, and constantly bear in mind that nothing is so beautiful as truth; truth alone is lovely and lasting. By this course only can we be made "beautiful for ever."

BURDOCK (*Arctium Lappa and Bardana*).—IMPORTUNITY.

THE Burdock is well known by all boys, to whom it is an inoffensive source of fun. They gather the seed-vessels, and throw them at their companions. The bristly hairs which cover the seed-vessels cling tenaciously to the dress, and require a little patience in detaching them. Thus the Burdock is a fitting emblem of that Importunity with which we are sometimes assailed by applicants, who seem determined not to take a refusal. It may also well be regarded as such from its pertinacious resistance of attempts to extirpate its roots even from good soil.

The generic name "Arctium" is given to this plant because of the brown hairy covering which resembles the shaggy skin of the bear. The hardened hooks at the end of the hairs hold so firmly to the coats of cattle, that as they separate, the seed-vessels are forced open, when the contents escape, and sow themselves! The plant has many useful properties.

BUTTERCUPS.—CHEERFULNESS.

EXCEPT the daisy, there is not a greater favourite than the Buttercup. Children of all ranks delight in it, and poets, calling to mind their early field pleasures, have not failed to speak of this wild flower, and have thus made a permanent record of the cheerfulness with which Buttercups inspired them. Campbell says,—

> " wildings of nature, I dote upon you;
> For ye waft me to summers of old,
> When the earth teemed around me with fairy delight,
> And when daisies and Buttercups gladdened my sight,
> Like treasures of silver and gold."

In the mind of another writer, with whose name we are unacquainted, Buttercups are associated with the pleasures of child-life, on their first appearance in spring,—

> " Again I feel my heart is dancing,
> With wildly-throbbing keen delight,
> At this bright scene of King-cups dancing
> Beneath the clear sun's golden light.
>
> Again I pluck the little flower,
> The first my childhood ever knew,
> And think upon the place and hour
> Where and when that first one grew ;
>
> And as I gaze upon its cup
> Shining with burnished gold,
> The faithful memory calls up
> How many a friend beloved of old ! "

And Miss Twamley, when she described her feelings about flowers in poetry, reveals vivid recollections of her pleasures in them as a child,—

> " Oh ! I can now recall th' unthrift delight
> That filled my basket and my tiny hand,
> With Buttercups that shone in burnished gold,"

and she thought that all children must have the same emotions on seeing them, for she calls them—

> " blest childhood's darling, the Buttercup,
> With bright rays gilt, as its flowers glance up."

We have not made any distinction as to the species, with respect to its emblematic use, because the whole genus is known by the common name of Buttercups, &c., and their appearance is sufficiently pleasing to render any species a fit emblem of Cheerfulness.

CABBAGE (*Brassica*).—PROFIT.

WE do not commonly associate flowers with Cabbages; though the flowers borne by some species are not displeasing. The genus is a very proper emblem of Profit, since there are many garden kinds of great value, of which the Cauliflower is esteemed by some persons to be "the finest flower the garden grows;" then the Turnip, Rape, and other agricultural sorts are extensively cultivated for profit, both as regards the tuberous roots and the succulent heads, as formerly at Rome the fields were covered with Cabbage for the like purpose. The French have a proverb, "*Fait ses choux gras*," which we may freely render, "He feathers his nest well," when they would imply that a man conducts his business well, and makes everything turn to his own advantage. One may acquire wealth by such a selfish mode if so resolved, but there is a certain book of great antiquity which calls it dangerous. "They that will (are determined to) be rich fall into temptation, and a snare, and into many foolish and hurtful lusts (longings), which drown men in destruction and perdition; for the LOVE *of money* is the root of all evils."

CANDY TUFT (*Iberis semperflorens*).—INDIFFERENCE.

THIS small shrub is an evergreen, and throughout the year we find it bearing its white and scentless bloom. When he collects the seeds, the gardener must put aside the flowers which cover them. In bearing fruit it does not fade, but preserves its leaves and flowers even in decay. The seasons appear to pass by this plant without affecting it. How different to the changes in nature generally, which beautiful spring produces:—

" See the young, the rosy Spring, gives to the breeze her spangled wing;
While virgin graces, warm with May, fling roses o'er her dewy way!
The murmuring billows of the deep have languished into silent sleep;
And mark! the flitting sea-birds lave their plumes in the reflecting wave;
While cranes from hoary winter fly to flutter in a kinder sky.
Now the genial star of day dissolves the murky clouds away;
And cultured field, and winding stream, are sweetly tissued by his beam.
Now the earth prolific swells with leafy buds and flowery bells;
Gemming shoots the olive twine, clusters ripe festoon the vine;
All along the branches creeping, through the velvet foliage peeping,
Little infant fruits we see nursing into luxury!"—MOORE's *Anacreon.*

Not so with the very cold and impassible Iberis, wherefore Eastern beauties made it the emblem of Indifference. They, indeed, are thought to have been the first inventors of the language of flowers, a language for the first time put prominently before the fair ladies of England, by Lady Mary Wortley Montague, who sent a Turkish love-letter from Pera to one of her friends in England, which contained the following floral emblems:—

46

" *Clove.*   You are as slender as this clove !
             You are an unblown rose !
             I háve long loved you, and you have not known it.

Jonquil.   Have pity on my passion !

Pear.   Give me some hope !

A Rose.   May you be pleased, and your sorrows mine !

A Straw.   Suffer me to be your slave !

Cinnamon.   But my fortune is yours !

Pepper.   Send me an answer ! "

Every flower, says her ladyship, represents a sentiment:
Letters of civility, friendship, and love, may be sent without
the use of ink. Anger, reproach, or news, may be conveyed
by these eloquent emblems.

THE CHERRY (*Prunes Cerasus*).—GOOD EDUCATION.

" Ye may simper, blush, and smile, and perfume the air awhile;
But sweet things, ye must be gone, fruit, ye know, is coming on ;
Then, oh then, where is your grace, when as cherries come in place ? "

HERRICK, while admiring Cherry-blossom, is anticipating
the time when the fruit will be ripe. Very pretty is the
Cherry-tree when in bloom. We found two splendid specimens of the wild Cherry growing in the boundary-fence
of our grounds, where, for the last eighteen springs we have
had the gratification of seeing its cheering white flowers,
with which it was literally covered all over, as we have sat

in our dining-room ; and therefore we can fully enter into the spirit of Barry Cornwall (by which *nom de plume* he is best known), in his address to the wild Cherry-tree :—

> " Oh,—there never was yet so fair a thing,
> By racing river or bubbling spring,—
> Nothing that ever so gaily grew
> Up from the ground when the skies were blue,
> Nothing so brave—nothing so free,
> As *thou*—my wild, wild Cherry-tree!
>
> Jove! how it danced in the gusty breeze!
> Jove! how it frolicked amongst the trees!
> Dashing the pride of the poplar down,
> Stripping the thorn of his hoary crown!
> Oak or ash—what matter to *thee?*
> 'Twas the same to my wild, wild Cherry-tree!
>
> Never at rest, like one that's young,
> Abroad to the winds its arms it flung,
> Shaking its bright and crownèd head,
> Whilst I stole up for its berries red—
> Beautiful berries! beautiful tree!
> Hurrah! for the wild, wild Cherry-tree!
>
> Back I fly to the days gone by,
> And I see thy branches against the sky,
> I see in the grass thy blossoms shed,
> I see (nay, I taste) thy berries red,
> And I shout—like the tempest loud and free,—
> Hurrah! for the wild, wild Cherry-tree !"

Cherry blossoms may be prettier on the cultivated tree, on account of the roseate tinge upon the petals. Both trees are, when blooming, very pleasing, but when the season for gathering fruit arrives there is a vast difference. Then the garden tree shows the effect of a Good Education, and the trainer's pains are well rewarded by a rich and delicious fruit. Such difference is there between an untaught person who presumes to prune our fruit-trees, and the educated fruit-grower, who has learned their various habits, and knows how to do his work. The former, if allowed to prune trees, will usually destroy all the fruit-bearing branches, while the latter cuts away those which only exhaust the tree, and retains such as will bear abundant and good fruit.

The tree, ornamental in flower, deserves our regard for its pleasant fruit, and is highly esteemed by the turner and cabinet-maker for the hardness of its wood.

THE CHASTE TREE (*Vitex agnus castus*).—COLDNESS. CHASTITY.

THIS is an autumnal shrub, bearing blue and white flowers in spikes of seven to sixteen inches in length. The dried leaves are very aromatic. For fanciful reasons it has had assigned to it the singular specific name *Agnus Castus*, and been made the emblem of Coldness and Chastity.

THE CHESTNUT TREE (*Castanea vesca*).—Do
ME JUSTICE.

" The Chestnut flowers
By thousands have burst from the forest bowers."—
HEMANS.

THE fruit of the Chestnut is contained in a green shell, covered over with prickles, which gives it a rough and unattractive appearance. This outward aspect causes persons who are not acquainted with the edible character of their contents to neglect or despise them. They are commonly roasted and then eaten ; but on the continent they are also boiled and ground into meal, which is made into bread, cakes, or puddings, hence it seems the fruit has a right to say to those who overlook its merits, Do me Justice. It is an excellent tree for hop-poles. In Kent and other hop-growing districts this is therefore almost exclusively cultivated for poles.

THE CHINA ASTER (*Aster Chinensis*).—VARIETY.

WHEN this species was first seen in our borders it was called the China Aster, because it came to us from China, and its flowers resembled the many radii of a star.

We are said to be indebted to a Missionary, one D'Incarville by name, who sent some seeds to the Jardin de Roi, about 1730.

The plants raised from the seeds sent by M. D'Incarville yielded only one variety, and flowers of uniform colour. Eventually, the velvety florets which surrounded the disc, were doubled, quadrupled, and varied indefinitely by cultivation. Some have thought, but erroneously, that the Chinese were acquainted only with the simple violet-coloured flower which had been sent to us. They have, in fact, all the sorts which attract our admiration, and they know how to make use of these varieties so as to form, by means of the China Aster, decorations which words cannot adequately describe. To prepare the flowers for this purpose, they grow them in pots; they then arrange them according to their colour and shades of colour; and with such a fine art that they display them as a continuous border, with the utmost harmony. "I wished," writes Madame de la Tour, "to form a similar decoration, a noted traveller having said much to me about them; but there was wanting to secure the full effect, a like profusion of flowers, the vast variety of shades in each colour, which they possessed, and, beyond these, that remarkable Chinese patience, which disregards every difficulty. Still, my little display gave gratification to all, and many were surprised as well as myself, that such decorations were not adopted in our gardens, and more especially in our floral fêtes."

As the emblem of variety, the China Aster owes its chief charms to successful culture. The skilful hand of the florist has surrounded her golden disc with all the colours of the rainbow. In like manner careful study and mental culture can develope great variety in the character of our natural endowments. Though majestic and brilliant in appearance, the China Aster does not presume to rival the rose, but follows after her when her charms have fled, as if she would console us for her regretted absence.

CINQUEFOIL (*Potentilla*).—BELOVED DAUGHTER.

THERE are many species of Potentilla, so named originally on account of its supposed potency in medicine. They all bear in common the English name " Cinquefoil," but our favourite species, we might say our choice favourite, among the whole range of our native plants, is the common Cinquefoil (*P. reptans*). This species is not met with everywhere; we were most pleased with it in the neighbourhood of Cambridge, where it somewhat abounds. Our appreciation of it is pretty fully expressed in the following lines, which first appeared in " Favourite Field Flowers:"—

"How gracefully the Potentilla throws
    Its trailing branches down the rude bank-side,
Until they kiss the wavelet as it flows
    O'er pebbles polished by the crystal tide;
    Nor there alone it grows, but far and wide
Its quinate leaves and golden blossoms lay,
And deck the borders of each rural way.

How beautiful its slender stem, imbued
    With rich fresh tinge of purple blush and green,
At intervals with fine-cut leaves indued,
    And bright-hued flower rising them between !
    No plant more elegant hath ever been
Within our native sea-girt island found,
'Mong those by which its hills and dales are crowned."

Of one species of Cinquefoil we have read that, in rainy weather, the leaves draw together, and incline over the flower, so as to form a kind of *parapluie*, or umbrella. A fanciful mind sees in this the act of a tender mother, carefully shielding a beloved daughter from impending calamities.

CLEMATIS.—ARTIFICE.

THE Clematis is a great favourite in our gardens, because of its mass of flowers and their delicious fragrance in autumn. It is a deciduous climber of very rapid growth, and, carefully trained over trellis work, or around windows, is very gracefully ornamental. The species have long been used to cover rustic arbours, whence probably their name "Virgin's Bower." Cowper addressed a few lines to one presented to adorn a garden seat, by that appellation,—

"Thrive, gentle plant! and weave a bower for Mary and for me,
And deck with many a splendid flower thy foliage large and free."

Keats mentions it by the same name,—

"The creeper, mellowing for an autumn blush;
And Virgin's Bower, trailing airily."

The chief of our garden kinds are *C. Florida*, a Japanese species, with whitish-yellow flowers; *C. Viticella*, with purple flowers from June to September; and *C. flammula*, an importation from France, which puts forth a profusion of white highly odoriferous flowers during the latter part of summer and until the frosty nights destroy its bloom. We have an indigenous species, *C. Vitalba*, not seldom found in chalk or limestone soils, in hedges and retired localities. This is known as "Traveller's Joy," probably because, by climbing up and about trees, its festoons form a leafy bower, which in the heat of a summer's day (with the thermometer* at 85°.5, as it has been this 20th of June, 1868, in the shade) may afford a comparatively cool shelter to the weary pedestrian rejoiced to find so welcome a resting-place.

The juices of different kinds of Clematis are very acrid, causing irritating inflammation if applied to the skin, and if continuously, ulceration. We are told that beggars use the juice to procure ulcerations, that they may expose their sores, and rouse the commiseration of the charitable, and obtain money. Cowper accuses gipsies of such artifices. He is describing a gipsy encampment, and, dilating upon their modes of gaining subsistence, adds,—

> "Great skill have they in palmistry, and more
> To conjure clean away the gold they touch,
> Conveying worthless dross into its place;
> Loud when they beg, dumb only when they steal.
>
> * * * * *
>
>   feigning sickness oft,
> They swathe the forehead, drag the limping limb,
> And vex their flesh with artificial sores."

The Clematis well represents Artifice on this account, but we would rather think of it as a graceful climber, affording a pleasant shade, and gratifying us with its very delicious fragrance.

* Radiating Thermometer on grass, exposed to the direct rays of the sun, stood at 148°.7 Fahr.

THE CLOVE TREE (*Caryophyllus aromaticus*).—DIGNITY.

THE Aromatic Clove Tree is a native of the Moluccas. It was brought into England in 1797, and there are specimens in English gardens. It requires a moist or bark stove for its cultivation. The fruit, which is well known to us from its use as a culinary spice, somewhat resembles a nail, wherefore it is called *Clous de Giroflier*, by our French neighbours. There are divers preparations from it sold by our druggists, which have the property of mitigating some of the many pains which we have to bear. The inhabitants of the Molucca islands are said to use cloves as marks of distinction. They distinguish their native notabilities by speaking of them respectively as having one, two, three, or four cloves, just as we speak of the titles of our aristocracy, the recapitulation of which at the funeral of men of renown, occupies considerable time. In the absence of this tree, its flowers and its fruit, from our gardens, the Clove Pink, whose fragrance puts us in mind of the spice, may be well substituted as the emblem of Dignity.

THE COLUMBINE (*Aquilegia vulagris*).—FOLLY.

THIS curious flower is not rare in a wild state in woods, plantations, and hedgerows. It is cultivated as a border-flower, when it frequently becomes double, and its colour varies from dark purple to crimson, pink, and white. It

55

often remains single. We brought a few seeds with us from Godalming, sowed them on a bank among common laurels, the Mahonia and other shrubs, and the plant has maintained its original position, uncared for, and has bloomed regularly every succeeding year for the last seventeen summers. It was this year quite white. There is only one solitary stem, with its seed-vessels now ripening, but it puts us in mind of its parent-plant, and of the beautiful spot in which that parent flourished. The plant seems to have been called Columbine from the resemblance of the flowers to doves, and Aquilegia on account of the inverted spurs being thought to resemble the talons of a bird of prey. The flower, as a whole, reminds some of the cap and bells worn by Columbine in a pantomime, and has been considered a meet emblem of Folly.

The Columbine was known to our early poets. Chaucer says—

"Come forth now with thin eyen Columbine;"

and Spenser speaks of two different coloured flowers,

"Bring hither the pincke and purple Cullambine;"

as a wild flower it has been mentioned as of three different tints,—

"In pink or purple hues arrayed, ofttimes indeed in white,
We see, within the woodland glade, the Columbine delight ;
Some three feet high, with stem erect, the plant unaided grows,
And at the summit, now deflect, the strange-formed flower blows."—

Field Flowers.

THE CORIANDER (*Coriandrum sativum*).—HIDDEN MERIT.

THE name of this annual was given to it on account of the odour of the leaves, which is offensive like that of the insect which the Greek word designates. The dried ripe seeds, however, are most agreeable in smell. They are aromatic and carminative, and on that account are compounded with some medicines to conceal their disagreeable taste and effects. The confectioner uses them in sweetmeats, and in some kinds of plum-bread. The Peruvians are fond of its flavour in most of their dishes.

The repulsive odour of the leaves tends to hinder the discovery of the great utility of the seeds; which, when their properties are known, deserve our high estimation. How often do we feel repelled by the plain, repulsive, or ugly countenance of persons, when we see them for the first time, and are disposed to murmur to ourselves,—

> " I do not like you, Doctor Fell !
> The reason why I cannot tell,
> But, I don't like you, Doctor Fell ; "

and yet, after a time, if circumstances have led to our knowing them better, how frequently has the ugliness become less repulsive, the plain face even pleasing, through the influence of the hidden wealth of mind, and heart, and character, then revealed, which erewhile was concealed from us by the apparent displeasing exterior of the casket !

57

CORN POPPY (*Papaver Rheas.*)—CONSOLATION.

THE several species of Poppy are showy in their appearance, and one yields the singular drug or medicine, opium, which, valuable in the hands of the skilful practitioner, is most injurious to those who have become addicted to its use as a stimulant. We cannot enter here into the consideration of the fearful consequences of indulging in it, nor of the mischief done by its too free administration as a medicine, in cases where there is no hope of ultimate recovery. We are, nevertheless, sensible of its great utility in lulling the sense of pain ; in procuring sleep for those who would otherwise be sleepless, through calamity, or adversity, or bitter sorrow, in whatever way produced ; a sleep beneficial, yet neither so refreshing, nor so strength-restoring, as that which nature brings to the wearied frame of the sound in health ; to those whose minds are content, and whose conscience is void of offence. It is as the inducer of sleep that the Corn Poppy is made the emblem of Consolation ; and justly so, for sleep is, indeed, the great healer of many ills, and the great consoler of many a sorrowing heart. Shakspeare puts into the mouth of King Henry IV. an apostrophe to sleep, which we can fully understand to have passed, in substance, through the mind of a monarch troubled with the cares of State in turbulent times :—

> " How many thousands of my poorest subjects
> Are at this hour asleep ! O sleep, O gentle sleep,
> Nature's soft nurse, how have I frighted thee,

That thou no more wilt weigh my eyelids down
And steep my senses in forgetfulness?

*   *   *   *   *   *

O thou dull god, why liest thou with the vile
In loathsome beds, and leavest the kingly couch?

*   *   *   *   *   *

Uneasy lies the head that wears a crown."

Sleep relaxes the animal frame, so that it becomes help-less, and the five senses are so dulled that it bears a close resemblance to the insensibility of the dead. Hence Sleep and Death are regarded as twin-brothers. When the hero Sarpedon fell in the plains of Troy, Apollo, at the bidding of Jove, went and forthwith drew the divine Sarpedon from amid the javelins, bore him far away, washed him in the flowing river, and anointed him with ambrosia, and wrapped around him an immortal robe; and anon

"To two swift-bearers gave him then in charge,
To Sleep and Death, twin brothers ; in their arms
They bore him safely to Lycia's wide-spread plain."

HOMER (*Lord Derby's Trans.*).

The species named at the head of this article seems to have been named Rheas with reference to Rhea, or Cybele, wife of Cronos, mother of Zeus, or Jove, and, therefore, "mother of the Gods." She was worshipped by the ancients, and repre-sented as wearing a wreath of Poppy-heads.

THE CORNELIAN CHERRY (*Cornus sanguinea*).— DURATION.

THE wood of this tree is said to be as hard as horn (*cornu*) ; hence its generic name. Virgil tells us that it was used in the manufacture of implements of war ; and it is related of Romulus, the mythic founder of Rome, that, when he had marked out the boundary of the embryo city, he hurled a javelin over Mount Palatine ; that the javelin shaft was of cornel wood ; that it penetrated the earth, took root, grew up, put forth branches and leaves, and thus became a tree ! This prodigy was regarded as a happy omen, foreshowing the strength and duration of the infant empire ! ! Surely the author of Baron Munchausen must have taken a hint from this.

The wood is applied to a variety of useful purposes. It is called Dogwood. As a shrub, it is a good emblem of Hardness and Duration; for in plantations where the lower branches have perished, there, even under the drip of trees, this will flourish and fill up the vacant spaces.

The Greeks worshipped Apollo, to whom they consecrated this tree, because he presided over works of talent. It is, therefore, an emblem worthy of adoption by all who are determined to cultivate literature, oratory, and poetry; since, if they would win the laurel leaf, it must be by patient enduring labour, in study and in persistent reflection.

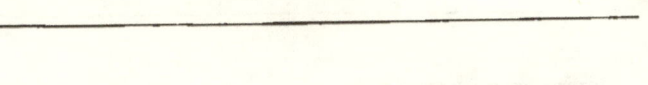

THE COWSLIP (*Primula veris*).—EARLY JOYS.

A FLOWER so profusely scattered over our meadows in the merry months of May and June, needs only to be named to recall to mind our early joys, when we roamed at will gathering Cowslips with eager delight, and breathing their delicious fragrance. How merrily did our great Shakspeare sing when he thought of them, and fancied fairies dwelt in their golden cups,—

> " Where the bee sucks, there lurk I ;
> In a Cowslip's bell I lie ;
> There I crouch when owls do cry."

Miss Taylor, in her verses entitled " Leafy Spring," betrays her fondness for these charming flowers,—

> " On pastures wide and green, upon a thousand stems,
> Fit for a fairy queen to wear for precious gems,
> Young Cowslips smile at earth and sky,
> With sweetest breath and golden eye."

But why should we say more of this beauteous remembrancer of the happiness of childhood? No one, who, at that golden age, spent any time in the country when it was in bloom, can have failed to partake of those early joys of which it is such an appropriate token.

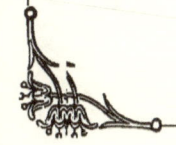

THE CROCUS (*Crocus vernus*).—PLEASURES OF HOPE.

THE Snowdrop is the emblem of Consolation, reminding us that the season is approaching when blooming flowers will again deck the earth in beautiful profusion ; with her attendant comes up the Crocus, which imparts to our hope of returning spring such emotions of pleasure, that it may well represent those agreeable sensations which pervade the mind when we see the purple, and golden, and violet-coloured flowers bursting through the earth, not seldom covered with snow, which gives additional zest to our gratification. Poets have at all times inwoven it in their verse : Homer speaks of "Crocus and Hyacinth," and Milton mentions them together in like manner ; Thomson associates it with the Snowdrop ;—

> "Fair-handed Spring unbosoms every grace,
> Throws out the Snowdrop and the Crocus first ;"

So, also, Miss Taylor, in speaking of the leafy spring,—

> "Above the garden beds, watched well by lady's eye,
> Snowdrops with milky heads peep to the softening sky,
> And welcome Crocuses shoot up,
> With gilded spike and golden cup."

To Miss Twamley's imagination the Crocus was a right royal flower,—

> "The regal Crocus, in purple and gold,
> Bursts with life from its leafy fold."

And elsewhere, fancying the Snowdrop to come forth at the call of the robin in his merry song, she writes,—

> " And presently the Crocus heard their greeting, and awoke,
> And donned with care her golden robe and emerald-coloured cloak ;
> * * * * * * *
> The Crocus brought her sisters too, the purple, pied, and white;
> And the redbreast warbled merrily above the flowercts bright."

Bernard Barton looked upon it as an emblem of the leaf which the dove brought to Noah in the ark, when hoping for the subsidence of the waters, and thus addressed it :—

> " Thine is the flower of hope, whose hue
> Is bright with coming joy."

So poets, and all who delight in flowers, have felt a gush of pleasure when these bright things have first presented themselves in the parterre, a promise of the coming spring.

THE CROWN IMPERIAL (*Fritillaria Imperialis*).—
POWER.

FRITILLARIA, the generic name of the chequered Daffodil, or Snake's-head Lily, was given to it from its resemblance to the Roman dice-box. Our indigenous species is called Meleagris, because its markings are like those of Guinea-fowl, hence we find people speaking of it as the Guinea-hen flower. Its tulip-shaped cup hangs down inverted, which has given rise to the absurd name of " The Drooping Young Man," in some parts of the country. It is a common plant in Norfolk and Suffolk, and we have met with it in Cambridgeshire. It was at one time so abundant near Kew, that a meadow between that royal residence and Mortlake, retains the appellation of Snake's-head Meadow. Into this genus was the Crown Imperial admitted. It was brought from Persia in 1596. It is very ornamental. The bright yellow flowers hang in an inverted position, the petals curling outwards and upwards, each flower closely resembling a turban. The flowers are studded round the stem, which is sometimes four feet high, and are surmounted by a cluster of rich green leaves. The general appearance of the plant in bloom might well suggest to Cowper to write,—

> " The Lily's height bespoke command,
> A fair Imperial Flower ;
> She seemed designed for Flora's hand,
> The sceptre of her power."

In each flower of the Crown Imperial has been observed several drops of fluid, which adhere to the bottom of the corolla until it is faded. Then the pedicles of the flowers raise themselves for the seeds to ripen. We are gravely told that "the performances of the six stamina are very curious. Now all are remote from the pistil; anon three approach at once to do it homage ; then the other three draw near for the same loyal purpose, when the former have retired ! ! "

CELERY-LEAVED CROWFOOT (*Ranunculus sceleratus*).—INGRATITUDE.

THE specific name of this plant, which is usually included under the common term " Buttercups," marks its pernicious properties. It is one of the most acrid of the genus, quickly causing great inflammation. It is used among other herbs, by vagabond mendicants, to produce ulcers in the legs, that indiscriminate almsgivers may commiserate, and give them money. Clare thus alludes to its ungrateful qualities,—

> " I wander out and rhyme;
> What hour the dewy morning's infancy
> Hangs on each blade of grass and every tree,
> And sprents the red thighs of the humble bee,
> Who 'gins betimes unwearied minstrelsy;
> Who breakfasts, dines, and most divinely sups
> With every flower save golden butter-cups,—
> On whose proud bosoms he will never go,
> But passes by with scarcely ' How do ye do?'
> Since in their showy, shining, gaudy cells,
> Haply the summer's honey never dwells."

Ranunculus sceleratus may be turned into the English words, the *detestable Crowfoot;* and since nothing is more common, and nothing more *professedly* detestable, than Ingratitude, it is a most fit emblem of that fault in human nature, a fault hateful in all, but still more hateful and heinous in a child. Shakspeare puts the following words into the mouth of King Lear,—

> " Ingratitude, thou marble-hearted fiend,
> More hideous when thou showest thee in a child
> Than the sea-monster ! "

because of the loving care and unlimited self-denial which parents exercise in promoting the happiness and future welfare of their offspring; even so we are told that the pernicious properties of this plant become intensified, by the culture and carefulness which the gardener may bestow upon it.

THE DAHLIA (*Dahlia superflua*).—MY GRATITUDE EXCEEDS YOUR CARE.

THIS favourite florist's flower, named in honour of Dahl, a Swedish botanist, is well known to every lover of Flora's subjects. It seems to have been imported into France about 1789, and its cultivation was nearly confined to that country until the peace of 1814. Then it was dispersed over Germany, Prussia, and Denmark; and found its way into England, where it soon became an object of great care and emulation, as well as a fruitful source of profit to the florist. Being a native of the very hot climate of Mexico, it was treated as if too tender for the comparatively cold climate of Europe; soon its constitution was tested in the greenhouse, and subjected there to an abundant supply of air; it was thus acclimatized by degrees, until it flourished in some localities for eight months, from the beginning of July to the end of February, in the open air of sunny France. Not less hardy is it, proportionately, in dear England, but here, so soon as the nights of Autumn become frosty, the beauty of its flowers fades, its herbaceous leaves and stems perish, and the tubers require to be exhumed and stored away as experience has taught the cultivator, if we would keep the living principle undestroyed until the succeeding spring. Martin has written of the Dahlia's endurance of various climates, thus :—

" Though severed from its native clime,
Where skies are ever bright and clear,

And Nature's face is all sublime,
    And beauty clothes the fragrant air,
    The Dahlia will each glory wear,
With tints as bright and leaves as green;
And winter, in his savage mien,
    May breathe forth storm,—yet she will bear
With all : and in the summer ray,
With blossoms deck the brow of day."

The Dahlia needs but little care after planting, yielding an abundance of flowers; but the amateur who has a genuine taste for beauty in his favourites, will, if he can possibly devote the necessary time to such a purpose, so train his plants, and reduce the number of their incipient bloom, as to produce the finest flowers which they are capable of bearing. And in so doing he will realize an enhanced pleasure in their possession, when like Longfellow's Ser Frederigo, he may

" Among the Dahlias in the garden walk
    Have left his guests;"

not fearing that they will complain of his negligence, in his absence, in the management of his parterre. On the contrary, when he shall have returned he will receive their gratulations on the beauty of his flowers, and on the rich reward he has secured in such a charming display of lasting bloom.

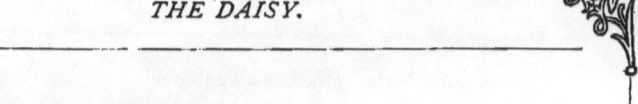

THE DAISY (*Bellis perennis*).—INNOCENCE.

WORDSWORTH calls the Daisy "the Poet's darling," and not without reason. By a prose poet it has been made the emblem of Innocence; here we have an account of the cause of this:—

"Malvina, bent over the tomb of Fingal, bewailed the valiant Oscar, and also Oscar's son, who died ere he saw the light.

"The virgins of Morven, to allay Malvina's grief, often came about her, honouring by their songs the death of the hero and the death of the new-born.

"'The hero is fallen,' they sang; 'he is fallen! and the sound of his arms has re-echoed over the plain; sickness, which takes away courage; old age, which discredits the deeds of the brave, can no more reach him; he is fallen! and the sound of his arms has re-echoed over the plain.'

"'Admitted to the palace of the shades where his ancestors dwell, he drinks with them of the cup of immortality. O beloved of Oscar! no longer shed tears of sorrow; the hero is fallen! he is fallen! and the sound of his arms has re-echoed over the plain.'

"Then with softer voice, they said again to her: 'Your child, who never saw the light, has never known the bitterness of life; his young soul, borne aloft on glittering wings, reaches with the first dawn of day the mansions of light. The souls of children, who, as well as he, have, without knowing sorrow, burst through the fetters of mortal life, reclined upon golden clouds, appear and open to him the mysterious gates of the fountain of Flora. There, the band of innocents, knowing nought of evil, are continually engaged folding up in sheaths, which cannot be seen by mortal eyes, the germs of flowers which every succeeding Spring shall cause to bloom. Every day, this infantine legion scatters over the earth those delicate buds, as the dews of rosy-fingered morning fall; a countless host of delicate hands inclose the rose in her bud, the grain in its sheath, the huge branches of an oak in a single acorn, and sometimes a whole forest in one invisible seed-vessel.

"'We have seen, oh, Malvina! we have seen the child which you vainly regret, cradled upon a fleecy cloud; he drew near us, and shed over our fields a harvest of new flowers! Look, oh Malvina! among them we distinguish one with a golden disc, surrounded as it were with plates of silver; a light soft purple tips its delicate rays; poised among the grass by a gentle breeze, one might fancy it to be a little child sporting itself in the verdant mead. Cease from tears, oh, Malvina! The hero is dead, clad in his armour, and the flower of your bosom has given a new flower to the hills of Cromla.'

"The sweetness of these songs allayed the grief of Malvina; she took her golden harp and sang in harmony with its notes, the song of the new-born.

"From that day forth, the maidens of Morven have consecrated the little Daisy to early infancy. It is, they say, the flower of Innocency; the flower of the new-born babe."

Cowper refers to the Daisy as the child's flower :—

"in the spring and play-time of the year
That calls the unwonted villager abroad
With all her little ones, a sportive train,
To gather king-cups in the yellow-mead,
And prank their hair with Daisies;"

and how intimately it is associated with child-life, is shown
by the effect of its appearance on a Missionary in India,
whose feelings James Montgomery poetized :—

" Thrice welcome, little English flower!
    Of early scenes beloved by me,
While happy in my father's bower,
    Thou shalt the blithe memorial be;
The fairy sports of infancy,
    Youth's golden age, and manhood's prime,
Home, country, kindred, friends, with thee
    Are mine in this far clime.

Thrice welcome, little English flower!
    I'll rear thee with a trembling hand;
O for the April sun and shower,
    The sweet May dews of that fair land,
Where Daisies, thick as star-light, stand
    In every walk!—that here might shoot
Thy scions, and thy buds expand,
    A hundred from one root!"

Miss Twamley had very joyous associations in her mind
with Daisies and the days of her childhood,—

" For one glance
Of wondering love we lifted to the vault
Of the o'er orbèd sky, have we not bent
Full many a gaze of pleased affection down

70

To the green field, starred over with its hosts
Of Daisies, countless as the blades of grass,
'Midst which they seemed to look and laugh at us?
* * * * * *
—Daisies, with their rose-tipped silvery rays
Spreading around the yellow boss within—
And some, most prized, that had not yet displayed
Their fairy circle, but emerging new
From their green hermitage, seemed as they blushed
Beneath the ardent sun's admiring gaze."

Burns says, in describing the contents of his Posy,—

" The Daisy 's for simplicity and unaffected air,"

the mark of that genuine purity and unsuspecting faith,
which is the essential characteristic of the best type of our
race, and which is seen in the child. Miss Twamley says
of it, —

" Rich in its ignorance is Infancy,
And every added year but makes more poor,
By added knowledge, childhood's guileless wealth,—
The wealth of an unblighted, unchilled soul."

Burns also calls it lowly, an epithet which the character
just spoken of may always claim,—

" All beneath th' unrivalled rose
The lowly Daisy sweetly blows."

We have seen that Wordsworth claims the Daisy as the
Poet's darling ; other poets have had the same fondness
for it ; Chaucer says,—

71

> "—of all the floures in the mede
> Than love I most these floures white and rede,
> Soch that men callen Daisies in our town,
> To hem I have so great affection,
> As I sayd erst, whan comen is the Maie,
> That in my bedde there daweth me no daie,
> That I n'am up and walking in the mede
> To see this floure ayenst the Sunne sprede;
> Whan it up riseth early by the morrow,
> That blissful sight softeneth all my sorrow."

and, as when, ere rosy-fingered morn tinged the eastern sky, he rose, so

> "As soon as ever the Sunne ginneth west
> To seen this floure, how it will go to rest,
> For feare of night, so hateth the darknesse,
> Here chere is plainly spred in the brightness
> Of the Sunne, for there it will unclose.

Shelley is reminded, by its ever-blooming, of the (to us) never-setting constellation, commonly known as Charles's-Wain :—

> "Daisies, those pearled Arcturi of the earth,
> The constellated flower that never sets."

Again, our poets commonly regard the Daisy as Nature's Favourite; thus Wordsworth,—

> "now my own delights I make,—
> My thirst at every rill can slake,
> And gladly Nature's love partake
> Of the sweet Daisy!"

Again he addresses it,—

"Bright flower, whose home is everywhere !
A pilgrim bold in Nature's care,
And all the long year through, the heir
    Of joy or sorrow,
Methinks that there abides in thee
Some concord with humanity,
Giv'n to no other flower I see
    The forest through !"

Burns in like manner,—

" Now Nature—
    —spreads her sheets o' Daisies white
    Out owre the grassy lea."

James Montgomery, in his verses entitled the Field Flower
(they should be called The Daisy), says of it,—

" —this small flower, to Nature dear,
    While moon and stars their courses run,
Wreathes the whole circle of the year,
    Companion of the sun.'

'Tis Flora's page :—in every place,
    In every season, fresh and fair,
It opens with perennial grace,
    And blossoms everywhere.

On waste and woodland, rock and plain,
    Its humble buds unheeded rise ;
The rose has but a summer reign,
    The Daisy never dies."

The profusion with which the Daisy is scattered everywhere is noticed by our poets. Milton writes of "medows
trim with Daisies pied" (variegated); Spenser, "the grassie
grounde with daintie Daisies dight" (dressed out); Miss

Taylor, "Daisies enamel (variegate) the plain;" Burns, "the bank, with Daisies all beset;" Shelley says,—

> "—the sinuous paths of lawn and moss,
> Which led through the garden along and across—
>   *   *   *   *   *   *
> Were all paved with Daisies;"

and Clare addresses the flower,—

> "Daisies, ye flowers of lowly birth,
> Embroiderers of the carpet earth,
> That stud the velvet sod;"

and Davors, who seems to have been a friend of Izaak Walton, and delighted in angling, speaking of those who preferred other sports, says,—

> "Let them that list, these pastimes still pursue,
> And on such pleasing fancies feed their fill;
> So I the fields and meadows green may view,
> And daily by fresh rivers walk at will,
> Among the Daisies."

and last, but not least, Mason Good, looking through nature up to nature's God, writes,—

> "Not worlds on worlds, in phalanx deep, need we to prove that God is here;
> The Daisy, fresh from winter's sleep, tells of His Hand in lines as clear:
> For who but He who arched the skies, and poured the day-spring's living flood,
> Wondrous alike in all He tries, could rear the Daisy's purple bud;
> Mould its green cup, its wiry stem, its fringèd border nicely spin,
> And cut the gold-embossèd gem that, set in silver, gleams within:
> And fling it unrestrained and free, o'er hill, and dale, and desert sod,
> That man, where'er he walks may see, the stamp of God?"

DAMASK ROSE (*Rosa Damascena*).—BEAUTY EVER NEW.

THE varieties of the Damask Rose are numerous. They are universal favourites. In May they begin and continue to bloom until Autumn. In France some varieties are in flower in every season of the year, whence they are called Roses de Quatre-Saisons, and on that account are the suitable emblem of Beauty Ever New. The Monthly Rose begins first, and continues the latest, to bloom in England, and therefore adequately supplies with us the place of the Rose de Quatre-Saisons. It flowers until checked by frosts, and if protected by glass, and aided by artificial heat, it will yield us its bloom up to Christmas.

DANDELION (*Leontoden taraxacum*).—ORACLE.

THE bright-hued Dandelion is known to all. It opens its petals to the earliest rays of the sun, a peculiarity Elliott has not forgotten to notice in enumerating "the wonders of the lane,"—

> "And here the sun-flower of the spring,
> Burns bright in morning's beam."

Moore alludes to its unfolding to the rays of the sun, and closing when they are withdrawn or intercepted,—

> "She, enamoured of the sun,
> At his departure hangs her head and weeps,
> And shrouds her sweetness up, and keeps

Sad vigils, like a cloistered nun,
Till his reviving ray appears,
Waking her beauty as he dries her tears."

The hour when the Dandelion opens and closes being known, it is a shepherd's time-piece ; Howitt, speaking of it, says,—

" Dandelion, with globe of down,
The schoolboy's clock in every town,
Which the truant puffs amain,
To conjure lost hours back again."

This globe of down is also the Oracle to every incipient lover of either sex. The youth not yet in his 'teens, meeting with one of them, begins to tempt his fate. He plucks the seed-stem from the plant, and puffs away the feathered sphere, alternately saying, "She loves me!" "She loves me not!" thinking of the pretty face and sparkling eyes which enchanted his throbbing heart at the last juvenile party. Then, according as one of these sentences is uttered as the last sphere leaves its native station, so is the answer to his anxious inquiry. The response is somewhat like those of the Delphic Oracle, very ambiguous, and capable of being interpreted as the inquirer desires. So he breathes gently or fiercely, softly or sharply, lest the response should dissipate the fond illusion which is adding a new and delicious charm to his young life.

DARNEL (*Lolium temulentum*).—VICE.

DARNEL is the emblem of Vice, because in warm climates it, together with the barren oat, grows so thickly in the fields as to choke good wheat. Its stem much resembles that of wheat, whence there is great difficulty in eradicating it, in an early stage of growth, without injuring the good corn. On this account, as well as for other reasons, it is thought that the word *tares* in a well-known parable should be *Darnel*, as giving a more accurate meaning. Shelley names it among offensive vegetation,—

"—the mandrakes, and toadstools, and docks, and Darnels,
Rose like the dead from their buried charnels."

DEAD LEAVES.—MELANCHOLY. SADNESS.

"The Dead Leaves strew the forest walk,
    And withered are the pale wild-flowers;
The frost hangs blackening on the stalk,
    The dewdrops fall in frozen showers."—BRAINARD.

NEAR the end of September we have abundant indications of the approach of winter. The trees have displayed their flowers; flowers have produced their fruit; the fruit, ripened by the summer's sun, has been gathered, and consumed, or stored up, or preserved for use in winter. Now the thick vapours are condensed upon our trees, and their leaves, once so vividly green, become various in hue, tawny, yellow, brown, lemon, and orange, as well as of divers shades of colour. Our planet has, in its course, drawn nearer to the sun, and the hours when we enjoy his light are daily lessened, the days are not so warm, the nights grow colder even to freezing, and the faded leaves fall continuously. The paths of garden, field, and forest are strewed with them. The beautiful Spring has gone, the brilliant Summer has fled, the changing Autumn is fast passing, and a sense of sadness pervades the mind, and a weight of melancholy depresses us, as the dead leaves remind us that "all that's bright must fade." Some friends we love must go on before, leaving us behind; while we in turn must pass away, and leave others who may grieve for us. Yet again shall Winter give way to Spring, the fields shall become verdant, flowers shall flourish, birds shall sing, all nature shall rejoice: so with sadness and melancholy; they too shall give way to consolation, and comfort, and be followed by happiness made more enjoyable by the contrast.

DITTANY (*Origanum Dictamnus*).—BIRTH.

WHEN Juno took charge of children at their birth, she assumed as a surname, Lucina (as bringing to light, *i.e.* life). At such times she wore a wreath of Dittany. The pleasant fragrance of this shrub, and its medicinal qualities, won the favour of the ancients and exact our regard. It is indigenous to Candia, or Crete. Its generic name signifies the Joy of the Mountain, a name it fully merits, since

its pretty spikes of flowers and pleasant perfume are indeed the joy of the places it thrives in. One species, commonly known as Marjoram, is a favourite culinary herb, rendering our dishes more relishing to the epicurean palate of the Englishman.

DODDER (*Cuscuta Europæa*).—BASENESS.

THE seeds of this genus, falling on the ground, lie dormant until Spring. They then form their slender stem and fibrous roots. If no other plant be near, these perish. It usually, however, attaches itself to some neighbouring plant, and entwines around it its slender branches. At intervals it protrudes a glandular apex, which soon puts forth a radicle acute enough to pierce the bark of the plant to which it adheres, and the fluids of which it absorbs. When this connexion is fully established, the original roots and stem of the Dodder die, and it becomes a true parasite, basely feeding on the vitals of the plant into which it has insinuated itself.

THE DOG ROSE (*Rosa canina*).—SIMPLICITY.

OF the Roses of June none afford such wide-spread pleasure as the Dog Rose. It does not confine itself to a few places, but decorates every hedge in the country with its simple beauty, and fills the air around it with most delicious perfume. When the first of its kind meets our eye, we are ready to exclaim with Mrs. Howitt,—

> "Welcome, oh! welcome once again,
>   Thou dearest of all the laughing flowers,
> That open their odorous bosoms when
>   The summer birds are in their bowers.
> There is none that I love, sweet gem, like thee,
>   So mildly through the green leaves stealing;
> For I seem as thy delicate flush I see,
> In the dewy haunts of my youth to be;
>   And a gladsome youthful feeling
> Springs to my heart, that not all the glare
> Of the blossoming East could awaken there;"

And at these times, when we think of, and look round upon, many of the beauties of Flora's kingdom, we are disposed to agree with her in preferring this flower, and say,—

> " —more than all, the sweet wild-rose,
>   Starring each bush in lanes and glades,
> Smiles in each lovelier tint that glows
>   On the cheeks of England's peerless maids."

It is a most fitting emblem of Simplicity, since it displays its charms, now of the faintest blush, anon of richer roseate hues, for the enjoyment and gratification of all, not confining its treasures to the enrichment of a select few.

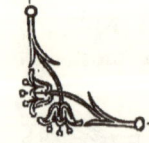

EBONY.—Blackness.

PLUTO, or Hades, is said to sit upon a throne of Ebony with his consort Persephone, at his court in Pandemonium. "He has a heart as black as Ebony," is not an uncommon expression, when one is spoken of who is believed to have done some great wickedness, or committed some act of gross deception. This would seem to have arisen from the fact, that Ebony is the heart-wood of a tree, the alburnum being of a pale hue, its foliage soft and of downy whiteness, while its flowers are beautiful and showy.

THE EGLANTINE (*Rosa rubiginosa.*)—POETRY.

THE Eglantine, or Sweet-briar Rose, is regarded as being specially the flower of poets. In the floral games it is awarded as the prize for the best production in praise of the pleasures of study, and the charms of oratory. But not only is it the Poet's flower, for, thriving in every situation, and universally admired and appreciated, both for its permanent fragrance, and the beauty and elegance of its simple flowers in their season, it is a most fitting emblem of poetry. How accurately does M. de Boisjolin speak of it in these lines,—

> " Fleur chère à tous les cœurs, elle pare à la fois
> Et le chaume du pauvre et le marbre des rois ;
> Elle orne tous les ans la beauté la plus sage ;
> Le prix de l'innocence en est aussi l'image ;"

and like it, genuine poetry, which appeals to the affections and sings of the feelings belonging to our common humanity, is fully appreciated, and therefore fully delighted in, as well by the cottager who becomes acquainted with it by hearing, as by crowned heads who read it at leisure in their splendid palaces.

To Cunningham, it was the Poet's flower *par excellence ;* all others were disregarded by him when that was at hand,—

> "Yes, every flower that blows, I passed unheeded by,
> Till this enchanting Rose had fixed my wandering eye;
> It scented every breeze that wantoned o'er the stream,
> Or trembled through the trees to meet the morning beam."

Landor, unacquainted, perhaps, with the many passages where poets have simply named the Sweetbriar, asks, as if complainingly,—

> "My briar, that smelledst sweet, when gentle spring's first heat
> Ran through thy quiet veins ;
> Thou that couldst injure none, but wouldst be left alone,
> Alone thou leavest me, and nought of thine remains.
> What, hath no poet's lyre o'er thee, sweet breathing briar,
> Hung fondly ill or well ?
> And yet methinks with thee, a poet's sympathy,
> Whether in weal or woe, in life or death, might dwell."

Our sweet Eglantine scatters its rich fragrance over, and beautifies the hedgerows and gardens of our transatlantic brethren. How warmly does the poet Brainard sing its praises,—

> "Our sweet autumnal western scented wind
> Robs of its odours none so sweet a flower,

In all the blooming waste it left behind,
As that the Sweetbriar yields it; and the shower
Meets not a rose that buds in beauty's bower
One half so lovely; yet it grows along
The poor girl's pathway, by the poor man's door.
Such are the simple folks it dwells among;
And humble as the bud, so humble be the song."

ENCHANTER'S NIGHTSHADE (*Circæa lutetiana*).—
SORCERY. WITCHCRAFT.

IN damp and humid places, where the superstitious mind
may imagine every kind of hideous reptile, and birds of evil
omen, to congregate; and plants and weeds of noxious properties to thrive; and where the wizened wizard and the
shrivelled hag, of face repulsive, might most fitly perform
their incantations; there does this plant delight to grow, as
"amid the mouldering bones and decayed coffins in the
ruinous vaults of Sleaford church, in Lincolnshire," and like
localities. Of its favourite habitat, Darwin, in his " Loves of
the Poets," thus writes,—

" Thrice round the grave Circæa prints her tread,
And chants the numbers which disturb the dead."

Moore, in the "Feast of Roses," introduces an enchantress,
who professes to have the power of charming back the strayed
love of Selim to Nourmahal, by means of flowers,—

" 'Tis the hour
That scatters spells on herb and flower,

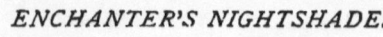

> And garlands might be gathered now,
> That, twined around the sleeper's brow,
> Would make him dream,—"

of Nourmahal, of course ; and further,—

> " Now, too, a chaplet might be wreathed
> Of buds o'er which the moon has breathed,
> Which worn by her, whose love has strayed,
>   Might bring some Peri from the skies,
> Some sprite, whose very soul is made
>   Of flowerets' breaths and lovers' sighs,
> And who might tell—"

how that love is to be restored ; and so

> " ' For me, for me,'
> Cried Nourmahal, impatiently,
> ' Oh ! twine that wreath for me to-night.'"

The enchantress does her bidding, and the result is that the royal lover's affections are again fixed upon the Sultana Nourmahal, the Light of the Harem.

If the enchanter's art always restored happiness to mortals, we might regret the loss of the race, which is now seemingly represented by professors of spirit-rapping. Since, however, the supposed power of the enchanter was used to stir up the author of all mischief, for some evil purpose, we cannot be sorry that the darkest days of superstition are ended. It was in those days that the enchanter's Nightshade was thought to have very wonderful properties. It is not of any value for good or ill.

THE EVENING PRIMROSE (*Œnothera biennis*).—
INCONSTANCY.

THIS ornamental flower is a native of North America. It is called the Evening Primrose because it opens its sulphur-coloured petals from six to seven p.m. Their mode of opening is remarkable. The petals are held together by hooks at the end of the flower-cup, whose segments separate first at the lower part, where the corolla may be seen for some time before its expansive force is strong enough to unhook the flower-cup at the top. When unhooked, the corolla opens out instantaneously as it were ; it then halts, taking time to spread out flat. The space of time occupied from the first disclosure of the corolla at the bottom, to its full expansion, is about half an hour. The corolla becomes flaccid during the next day, more or less quickly, as the atmosphere is hot and dry, or cold and moist.

Bernard Barton has set this flower in poetry,—

> "Fair flower, that shunn'st the glare of day,
>   Yet lov'st to open, meekly bold,
> To evening hues of sober grey,
>   Thy cup of paly gold ;
> Be thine the offering, owing long,
>   To thee, and to this pensive hour,
> Of the brief tributary song,
>   Though transient as thy flower."

The quickly blooming and speedy fading of this flower makes it a good emblem of Inconstancy.

85

A FEATHERY REED.—INDISCRETION.

WE are told that Pan and Apollo once contended with the flute and the lyre for pre-eminence in music, and made choice of Midas, King of Phrygia, to award the palm. He preferred the music of Pan to that of Apollo, whereupon the god of the silver-bow made the king's ears as an ass's ears. Midas hid them under his Phrygian cap, so that no one but his hair-dresser knew of the change. The man, harassed by the discovery, feeling that he could not keep it secret, and dreading the consequences to himself should he reveal it, dug a hole in the ground, and whispered into it the words, " Midas has ass's ears," as if he would bury it there. He then filled up the grave of the secret, on which a Feathery Reed grew up, and, as it waved about in the breeze,. it seemed to betray continually the buried secret, waving forth the words, " Midas has the ears of an ass ! "

FENNEL (*Anethum fœniculum*).—STRENGTH.

THE gladiators in training for exhibition used to mix Fennel with their food, for the purpose of stimulating their energies. Successful gladiators were crowned with a garland of Fennel, after the sports were concluded. It is now used by us for culinary purposes, giving a pleasant flavour to sauces served with salmon and mackerel. It forms a pretty garnish to these fish. The seeds are a strong carminative, and great quantities are annually imported from France for use in medicine.

FERN.—SINCERITY.

" The Foxgloves and the Fern, how gracefully they grow,
   With grand old oaks above them, and wavy grass below !
   The stately trees stand round, like columns fair and high,
   And the spreading branches bear a glorious canopy
   Of leaves, that rustling wave in the whispering summer air,
   And gaily greet the sunbeams that are falling brightly there."—
                                                Romance of Flowers.

WHEN the forest glades are bordered with Ferns in the
beauteous days of summer, these graceful forms of vegetable
life make a useful carpet.   Open to the lovely sky, mottled
over with clouds, amid which the glowing sun passes on his
glorious way, yet screened by a leafy canopy, such spaces
afford most pleasing resorts for the pic-nic party.   There may
ministering maidens and waiting gentlemen spread the cloth ;
set forth the savoury viands, the generous and sparkling
wines, and the various fruits of the season ; and then, seated
or reclining upon the obliging Fern, partake of the refreshing
collation.   How pleasantly passes the time on such occasions,
and how swiftly ! and then the freedom of such a reunion, the
desire to please, the lovely weather, the generous and delicate
refection, unlock the closed heart of those usually most
reserved.   Then hidden feelings show themselves ; thoughts,
at other times concealed, escape through the ivory inclosure
and ruby lips ; for the most part, they who are present are
then sincere, though in their sincerity sentiments may become
known which dispel some fond yet vain illusion, which must

87

no longer be cherished. Yet so much that is delightful is associated with these red-letter days, that we are bound to say with Miss Twamlay,—

> " The green and graceful Fern, how beautiful it is!
> There's not a leaf in all the land so wonderful I wis.
> Have ye ever watched it budding, with each stem and leaf
>   wrapped small,
> Coiled up within each other like a round and hairy ball?
> Have ye watched that ball unfolding each closely nestling curl,
> And its fair and feathery leaflets their spreading forms unfurl?
> Oh! then most gracefully they wave in the forest, like a sea,
> And dear as they are beautiful are those Fern leaves to me."

FIR TREE.—ELEVATION.

> " Those lofty Firs, that over-top
> Their ancient neighbour, the old steeple tower."—
>   WORDSWORTH.

THE Firs are a hardy family of trees, growing in the coldest regions and high situations, and attaining a height of from twenty to one hundred feet. They also grow with considerable rapidity. The " Wellingtonia gigantea," so named by the late Dr. Lindley, and designated by him "the monarch of the Californian forest," is a magnificent cone-bearing tree. One specimen was found on the Sierra Nevada, measuring 450 feet from its head to its root! This tree grows well in our climate. Young trees may be purchased at small cost; its ramification is pleasing; its verdure of agreeable tint; and its growth quick. All the Fir tribe are more or less useful as timber. Whether we consider it as thriving in lofty regions, as growing to great heights, or its high estimation as a timber-making family, it is most deservedly the emblem of Elevation.

FLAX (*Linum usitatissimum*).—I AM SENSIBLE OF YOUR KINDNESS.

> " How sweetly blooms
> Upon the slopes the azure-blossomed Flax."—
> CARRINGTON.

USITATISSIMUM! Most useful indeed is the Flax, which, Carrington tells us, blooms upon the slopes of the wilds of Dartmoor. It has been cultivated from the earliest ages on account of its valuable fibres, the raw material used in the manufacture of linen and other useful articles. Of it the rich lace which is so ornamental to the fair sex, is made. When the goods manufactured from it are worn out by use, the rags are converted into the best writing and drawing papers.

Not only is the fibre of the Flax exceedingly useful, but also the seed, which is used as food in its whole state. It is made into linseed cake, invaluable for feeding cattle, and in its manufacture a rich oil is expressed, highly prized by the artist, the ordinary painter, and the veterinary surgeon. It also supplies rape oil and the colza oil, which yield an artificial light so mild and agreeable in our sitting-rooms. We are, in fact, so deeply indebted to this plant that we must allow it to be a very appropriate emblem of the sentiment, " I am sensible of your Kindness."

THE FLOWERING FERN (*Osmunda regalis*).—Reverie.

THIS is the finest of our native Ferns. It is sometimes called the royal Fern. Its generic name, Osmunda, is supposed to be that of a goddess, queen of Thor, a Celtic divinity, and was applied to this plant for its alleged virtue in medicine. One of its fancied properties is to inspire those under its influence with dreams of great prophetic force, whence it is made the emblem of Reverie. This Fern grows in the most retired spots, in the midst of deep forests, as in the royal forest of Delamere, Cheshire ; and on vast bleak moors, as at Hind Head, a few miles from Godalming, Surrey. Wordsworth speaks of its retiring propensities—

> " Fair Ferns and flowers, and chiefly that tall Fern
> So stately, of the Queen Osmunda named,
> Plant lovelier in its own retired abode
> On Grasmere's beach, than Naiad by the side
> Of Grecian brook, or lady of the mere,
> Sole sitting by the shores of old romance ; "

so that its habitat, wherever that may be, is exactly suited to quiet musing, and those fits of abstraction which we are accustomed to speak of simply as a Reverie.

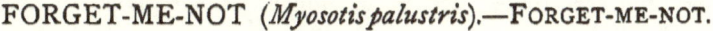

FORGET-ME-NOT (*Myosotis palustris*).—FORGET-ME-NOT.

"That name, it speaks in accents dear of love, and hope, and joy,
  and fear;
It softly tells an absent friend that links of love should never rend ;
Its whispers waft on swelling breeze, o'er hill and dale, by land and
  seas,   Forget-me-not!

Gem of the rill ! we love to greet thy blossoms smiling at our feet.
We fancy to thy flow'ret given a semblance of the azure heaven ;
And deem thine eye of gold to be the star that gleams so brilliantly."

THE Myosotis is nowhere seen, perhaps, in greater beauty
and abundance than on the borders of a small stream in
the environs of Luxembourg. The country people call this
streamlet the Fairies' Bath, or the Cascade of the Enchanted
Oak; these two names seem to have been given to it on
account of the beauty of its source, which it issues from
with a murmuring sound, at the foot of an oak tree as old as
the hills. Its waters bound along, at first, from cascade to
cascade, under a long covering of verdure, which they leave
only to flow gently through an extensive meadow. There
they seem to the delighted eye like a thread of silver. Part
of the bank is covered with a thick border of Myosotis,
whose pretty flowers are, in the month of July, of a bright
celestial blue. Then they bend down, as though they took
pleasure in admiring themselves in the crystal stream, the
purity of which cannot be surpassed. Ofttimes do the young
girls go down from the city, on holidays, to dance by the
side of the river. There, while weaving wreaths of the flower

it nourishes, we might fancy they were so many nymphs cele-brating accustomed sports in honour of the naiad of the enchanted oak.

Though every one knows why this pretty flower is used to express the wish, "Forget-me-not," we must here repeat the story :—Two lovers, on the eve of marriage, were walking on the banks of the Danube. A flower, blue as the deepest sky, swung upon the waves, which seemed ready to bear it away. The young lady admired its beautiful colour, and bewailed its impending destiny. The affianced bridegroom leaped into the stream, seized the blooming stem, and sunk engulfed in the flowing waters. It is said that, with a last effort, he threw the flower on the bank, and at the moment of his disappear-ance for ever, cried out, "Love me ; Forget-me-not !"

> " Pour exprimer l'amour ces fleurs semblent éclore ;
> Leur langage est un mot, mais il est plein d'appas.
> Dans la main des amants elles disent encore :
> Aimez-moi ; ne m'oubliez pas !"

This, the great Water Scorpion Grass, as a poetical writer, whose name we do not know, has said—

> " By rivulet, or spring, or wet road-side,
> That blue and bright-ey'd flow'ret of the brook,
> Hope's gentle gem, the sweet ' Forget-me-not,'"

is very ornamental. The blue of its petals is brilliant, and in the centre is a yellow eye, from which white lines radiate. Other species of the grass are smaller, are often mistaken for this, and, in the absence of the identical flower, may well be regarded as emblematical of the same sentiment.

FRAXINELLA (*Dictamnus F.*).—FIRE.

FRAXINELLA, the specific name, was given to this plant because its leaves closely , resemble those of the Ash (Fraxinus). If you rub the plant with your fingers it will emit a lemon scent; if you bruise it, the fragrance will be balsamic. The footstalks of the flowers are supposed to contain this fine scent. They are studded with glands of a rusty red, which exude a resinous or viscous fluid. This fluid exhales in vapour, and may be seen to take fire in dark places. It is alleged that when the day has been very hot and dry, and the evening damp, this exhalation is so inflammable as to ignite if a lighted bougie be brought near the plant.

FUMITORY (*Fumaria officinalis*).—HATRED.

A PRETTY weed, whose leaves smell rather disagreeable. The taste of the plant is somewhat bitter and saline, and is so offensive to the palate that it has been called by the French, *Fiel de terre*, and appropriated as the emblem of Hatred.

GARDEN WALL-FLOWER (*Cheiranthus cheiri*).— LASTING BEAUTY.

THE Greeks delighted in flowers, but were unacquainted with the art of cultivating and improving them; they received them as the wild gifts of nature. With the arts of

Greece, the Romans took up the taste for flowers, and their love of floral wreaths was so great that the use of certain flowers was prescribed for special purposes. These rulers of the then known world cultivated both violets and roses, and whole fields, covered with these flowers, soon encroached on the domain of Ceres. The valiant Gauls were long without the delicacies of life; their warlike hands disdaining even the use of the plough. With them, the garden was the territory of the mistress of the family, and contained nothing but aromatic plants and potherbs. In time their manners became softened, and Charlemagne, the terror of his foes and the father of his own people, was fond of flowers. He recommends the culture of the lily, the rose, and the wall-flower. Exotic flowers were not introduced amongst us until the thirteenth century. In the time of the Crusades, our warriors brought many new kinds from Egypt and Syria. The monks, at that time the only skilful cultivators of the soil, took care of them. They soon gave a pleasing charm to their quiet retreats; thence they spread over our parterres, and became our chief festal decorations, and the luxury of our castles and halls. Still the rose remains the queen of our groves, and the lily the king of our vales. The rose does not last long, and the lily passes away almost as quickly. The Wall-flower, less graceful than the rose, less superb than the lily, has a more lasting beauty; a difference which Moir has noted:

"Rich is the pink, the lily gay, the rose is Summer's guest;
Bland are thy charms when these decay—of flowers, first, last, and best!
These may be gaudier in the bower, and statelier on the tree;
But Wall-flower, loved Wall-flower, thou art the flower for me!"

94

For the greater part of the year the Wall-flower displays its orange, yellow, and red pyramidal bloom, which scatters continually a most agreeable fragrance, and these render the flower acceptable to all.   It gives a charm to the garden of the noble, and the flower-pot of the lowliest who cherish it with the fondest care.   It claims of right, which no one can dispute, to be the emblem of Lasting Beauty.

GATHERED FLOWERS.—WE DIE TOGETHER.

IT is well known how soon a mass of flowers, or fruit, or vegetables, decomposes the air, and renders it unfit for respiration, producing sickness and death.

This fact has suggested to a German writer, Freiligrath, a touching sketch, which he calls, "The Revenge of the Flowers."

"Returning from a botanical excursion, two young girls enter their home, close the windows, lie down and fall asleep. At their feet, in a basket, is seen the flowers which they have collected.   How indiscreet! where is their mother? who will warn them of the danger which surrounds them? Already the air is being decomposed, the atmosphere of the small apartment is heavy and unfit to breathe, and the youthful maidens weighed down by it writhe about unconsciously on their couch.   Suddenly, from amid the basket of flowers, rise up the spirits of the narcissus and the tuberose! They appear as two light nymphs dancing and whirling about, meanwhile chanting ominous words: 'Young maidens! young maidens! why have you deprived us of life? Nature gives

us but a day, and you have shortened it! Oh! how sweet
was the dew! how radiant the sun! and yet we must die!
but we will be avenged.' Thus chanting, the two nymphs,
continually whirling about and bewailing their fate, draw
near the young maidens' couch, and breathe over their faces
their poisonous exhalations. Poor children! Mark their
livid cheeks! their pale lips! their arms closely interwoven!
Alas! their heart has ceased to beat; they no longer breathe
the breath of life; they are dead together. The flowers are
avenged!"

GERMAN IRIS (*Iris germanica*).—ARDOUR. FLAME.

> " The azure fields of heaven were 'sembled right
> In a large round, set with the flowers of light :
> The flowers-de-luce, and the round sparks of dew
> That hung upon their azure leaves, did show
> Like twinkling stars, that sparkle in the evening blew."—
>
> FLETCHER.

THE German Iris is a plant which the peasants of that
country delight to cultivate on the tops of their cottages.
When the air gently waves about its beautiful flowers, and
the sun lights up their petals with mingled tints of gold, and
purple, and azure, one might say that bright and perfumed
flames glance upon the rustic roofs. No doubt this appearance
has caused the name *Flamme* to be given to this flower.

Three *Flower-de-luce*, or *Fleur-de-lis*, two and one, *or*, on a
shield *azure*, is the royal arms of France. It fitly speaks of
the ardour and enthusiasm which are peculiarly characteristic
of the inhabitants of *La belle France*. It is also a universally

admired decoration in ecclesiastical art, in which it is figured in great variety of form, but so faithfully representing the original as in no case to be mistaken. May it not in all places, so used, call to our minds that ardour and warmth of devotion which should mark all our religious observances?

GERMANDER SPEEDWELL (*Veronica chamædrys*).— FAITHFULNESS.

THERE are many species of this genus, but not one exceeds in beauty the little Germander Speedwell, which is very common in our hedgerows. Its pretty blue flowers grow in masses; and so much is it admired that it is introduced into our gardens, where it grows longer and blooms for a more lengthened period than in its wild state; but in this condition it rarely survives more than one year, and therefore is treated as an annual, and as such far surpasses many exotics, Its generic name is Greek, and is said by some to signify, Faithful Likeness.

GLASSWORT.—PRETENSION.

THE different species of this useful plant grow most abundantly by the sea, in salt marshes, and yield the barilla of commerce, so valuable in the manufacture of soap. It is also used in the production of glass, whence its common name. A lively fancy has compared it to one who, with some pretension to beauty, smitten with her own charms, delights in admiring her reflected image, since this pretty plant droops over the crystal stream near which it grows.

GLYCINE (*G. sinensis*).—YOUR FRIENDSHIP IS PLEASING AND AGREEABLE TO ME.

THE Glycine is an elegant creeper. The Chinese have made it the emblem of a tender and delicate friendship. That it may thrive with success, this plant needs to be supported, and sheltered under a wall with a south aspect. Its beautiful pale blue flowers, arranged in long pendulous branches like the laburnum and the acacia, bloom in succession during the summer; but it is in the month of April, especially, that they unfold themselves on all sides, and spread over the largest trees their perfumed wreaths. Then they cover our walls, they surround our windows, they form bowers, and fall down again like a shower of flowers from the roofs of our houses. They comply with all the caprices, and yield to all the demands, of those who cultivate them with care and attention.

We see that this plant is yielding, agreeable, and gentle, like friendship; and to preserve it, what does it require? That which the heart lavishes on a friend,—tenderness and attention.

GOAT'S RUE (*Galega officinalis*).—REASON.

THE juice of this plant was at one time used to tranquillize patients suffering mental delirium, and to recall the wandering faculties, whence it has been made the emblem of Reason. It is now of no repute as a medicine, but the species are cultivated and are handsome border flowers.

GOOSEFOOT (*Chenopodium Bonus Henricus*).—GOODNESS.

THE people have given the name of their best beloved King to a wholesome and useful plant, which grows within their reach, and which, in some sort, seems to belong to them exclusively. *Le Bon Henri* needs no cultivation in France, but flourishes everywhere along walls and thickets. It is at once the asparagus and spinach of the poor. Happy, a thousand times, is the king who merits such a simple homage!

GRASS.—USEFULNESS.

THE wisdom and beneficence of the great Creator of the universe is most plainly seen in the way in which His creatures are provided for. When the earth emerged from the abyss of waters, then, first of all vegetable life, Grass was bid to grow and clothe its surface. Then, when cattle, and fowls of the air, and creeping things were created, it was declared that for them was given every green herb for meat. Thus has grass from the beginning been the principal supply for them, and is the most common form of vegetation, whereon the cattle upon a thousand hills have fed, and grown, and multiplied, stocking the world with the vast amount of food now required by the millions upon millions of human beings who people it. What then can be more useful than grass in its many varieties? and what is more pleasing to look upon than the verdure with which it clothes our hills and

H 2

dales, our meadows and downs? Surely nothing. It has, therefore, most deservedly been adopted as the emblem of Usefulness.

GRASS-LEAVED GOOSE-FOOT (*Chenopodium altissimum*).—I DECLARE WAR AGAINST YOU.

THIS plant bears some resemblance to the pyramidal cypress. In some parts of Italy, of which country it is a native, the offering to any one the stems or stalks of it is regarded as an insult.

GREEK VALERIAN (*Polemonium cæruleum*).— RUPTURE.

PLINY records that the generic name Polemonium was given to a plant, because several kings disputed the honour of having discovered its virtues, and carried their disputes to such an extent as to try to settle them by an appeal to arms. It was also called Chilodynamia on account of its remarkable excellence. Pliny's plant is unknown now, but the name is borne by a pretty blue border flower, of easy culture and long known to the florist.

GUELDER ROSE (*Viburnum opulus*).—GOOD NEWS.

THIS is indigenous, and not uncommonly found in moist places in various parts of Great Britain in June and July. It is, however, better known as the Snowball Tree, which forms a pleasing addition to our groves with the lilac, the laburnum, and the crimson thorn. Under cultivation, the corollas of the flowers have expanded to almost as large a size as those of the radiating ones in the wild plant, and the cymes have become globose, whence it has obtained the common name. It is thus, as it were, possible to provide a snowball at Midsummer in payment of quit-rent to the sovereign, by the noble holder upon whom such terms are said to have been imposed.

The following legend accounts for the origin of the Guelder Rose.

A young damsel, scarcely fifteen years of age, died. Her spirit hovered about her dwelling when in life. She could not resolve to abandon, even for celestial regions, the fields she had so dearly loved. Of a sudden her guardian angel appeared to her. Desirous of fulfilling her wishes, he asked whether she would like to be transformed into a flower, and gave her the choice as to its kind. "Then," said he, "you will live in the garden or the meadow!" and looking round upon the different flowers of the land, added, "Would you wish to be a tulip?" "No," she said, "for the tulip has no fragrance." "A lily?" "The lily elevates herself above other flowers." "A rose?" "She bears thorns which cause pain." "A splendid camellia?" "No, no," suddenly exclaimed the spirit of the young damsel; "but, since it is permitted me to make my choice, I should like to be a Guelder Rose." "What!" cries the angel in astonishment, "do you desire to be in bloom when all nature seems dead? Think of the icy winds of winter; they will drive against you, and you will die without having felt the caresses of the gentle zephyr!" "Be it so," was the reply; "I shall live only for a day, but in that day I shall announce the coming Spring!"

We are not told in what way the flower was allowed to change the season of blooming from winter to summer.

HAWTHORN (*Cratægus oxyacantha*).—HOPE.

"Hope in the Hawthorn lay."—TWAMLEY.

THERE is no tree or shrub which we observe more closely in the early spring than the Hawthorn. We notice its swelling buds enlarging daily until the leaves unfold themselves. Here and there along the hedgerows patches of foliage are in advance of the rest. In sheltered places, some several feet in an enclosure may be quite verdant, while scarce a leaf has opened out elsewhere. Then come the bunches of flower buds, followed in due time by the sweet-scented flowers. While this change is taking place in the Hawthorn, from its foliation to its blooming, all Nature has been rousing herself into active life. An abundance of flowers cheer our hearts. Sweet concerts of birds ring in our ears. The redbreast, the finches, the blackbird, and thrush, have charmed us with their various notes, and we remember how they destroy many enemies to our fruits. Then the swallow, and the martin, and the cuckoo foretell us of sunny days, of verdant meads, of golden corn, of glorious fruits, which are to be showered into our lap. We welcome with delight, though not in so demonstrative a manner as our forefathers, the 1st

of May.   In the days of Chaucer (A.D. 1328–1400) it was
the custom to go a-Maying, for, says that poet:

> " —forthe goeth alle the Courte, bothe moste and leste,
> To fetch the flowirs freshe, and braunche and bloome,
> And namely Hawthorne brought both page and groome,
> With freshe garlantis partly blew and white ;"

and Spenser (A.D. 1553–1599) :

> " Youngthes folke now flocken in everie where
> To gather May buskets and smelling brere ;
> And home they hasten the postes to dight,
> And all the kirk pillours eare day-light
> With Hawthorn buds."

Herrick (born A.D. 1591) recounts very sweetly the festivi-
ties of May-day, and, as reproving his mistress for not rising
early on so joyous a morning, says :

> " There's not a budding boy or girle, this day,
> But is got up, and gone to bring in May.
> A deale of youth, ere this, is come
> Back, and with white thorn laden home."

Here and there May-day is still observed.   The May-pole is
decked with garlands of flowers ; the May Queen is chosen
and crowned.   The young dance upon the village-green, and
flirt or coquet, as in days of yore; while they whose days
for dancing are fled, sit upon the benches or chairs under the
shady foliage, recounting what May-day was in *their* time.
Goldsmith, in his " Deserted Village," makes mention of

> " The Hawthorn bush, with seats beneath the shade,
> For talking age and whispering lovers made ! "

a favourite seat for lovers, of which Burns is not unmindful :

> " If Heaven a draught of heavenly pleasure spare,
>   One cordial in this melancholy vale,
>   'Tis when a youthful, loving, modest pair,
>   In other's arms breathe out the tender tale,
>   Beneath the milk-white thorn that scents the evening gale ; "

full of hope of many happy days to come, as they wend their way through this chequered life, which they have resolved to do together.

Shakespeare asks :

> " Gives not the Hawthorn bush a sweeter shade
>   To shepherds looking on their silly sheep
>   Than doth a rich embroidered canopy ,
>   To kings, that fear their subjects' treachery ? "

Milton regards it as the favourite shade of the same rustic character :

> " And every shepherd tells his tale
>   Under the Hawthorn in the dale."

The poets are ever mindful of it.   Kirke White speaks of

> " The mossy seat beneath the Hawthorn's shade,"

and inviting " Contemplation " personified to accompany him, says, we

> " — on the upland stile embowered
>   With fragrant Hawthorn, snowy flowered,
>   Will sauntering sit."

Miss Twamley writes :

> " Come, let us rest this Hawthorn-tree below,
> And breathe its luscious fragrance ere it flies,
> And watch the tiny petals as they fall
> Circling and winnowing down our sylvan hall ; "

and Elliott calls upon his friend, saying :

> " — walk with me where Hawthorns hide
> The wonders of the lane ; "

and all our poets are in harmony with respect to the charms of the Hawthorn, and might join in Miss Taylor's words :

> " I love the pleasant Spring, when buds begin to push,
> And flowers their nosegays bring to hang on every bush,
> Till stores of May, with snowy bloom,
> Fill the young hedgerows with perfume."

The Troglodytes, whose simple manners remind us of the golden age, used to cover the friends whom death had taken with branches of Hawthorn, since they looked upon death as the morning of a life where there would be no more parting. Longfellow well expresses this idea :

> " There is no death ! what seems so is transition ;
> This life of mortal breath is but a suburb of the life Elysian,
> Whose portal we call death."

At Athens, the fair young friends of a bride carried branches of the Hawthorn at her nuptials ; and the altar of Hymen was lighted up with torches made of the wood of this tree, which has ever been regarded as the emblem of Hope. It tells us of bright days at hand ; it held out to the beautiful Greek the promise of happiness in marriage ; and to the simple Troglodytes it spoke of life eternal.

THE HAZEL (*Corylus avellana*).—RECONCILIATION. PEACE.

TIME was when the human race had no common bond of union. Deaf to the cries of nature, the lover abandoned his mistress; the mother snatched from her child the wild fruit with which he sought to satisfy his hunger. If misfortune united them for a moment, the sight of an oak laden with acorns, or of a beech-tree bearing abundant mast, made them enemies. Then the world was filled with woe. There was neither law, nor religion, nor intelligible language. Man understood not his nature; his reason slept, and he was oft as cruel as the most ferocious beasts, whose howlings he imitated.

The gods took pity upon mankind; Apollo and Mercury prepared gifts and came down upon earth. The god of harmony received from the son of Maïa a tortoise-shell with which he made a lyre, and gave to Mercury, in exchange, a hazel-rod, which had the power to inspire with a love of virtue, and to reconcile hearts divided by hatred and envy: thus provided, the two sons of Jupiter presented themselves to men. Apollo sang forthwith of that Eternal Wisdom which made the world; he told them how the elements were produced, and how charity unites by its gentle influence all created beings; and taught his hearers that they must appease the anger of the gods by prayer. At his voice you might have seen mothers, pale and trembling, draw near him, holding their little infants in their arms; hunger ceased;

revenge fled from every heart. Then Mercury touched men with the wand given to him by Apollo. He set free their tongue, and taught them to express thoughts by words. He told them that union was strength, and that nothing could be obtained from the earth without mutual aid. Filial piety and the love of country sprung into existence, at his teaching, to unite the human species ; and he made commerce the bond which should bring all the world into harmony. His last thought was the most sublime, for it was sacred to the gods, and showed men how they might approach them in character by the exercise of love and beneficence.

Decorated with two light wings, and surrounded by serpents, the Hazel-wand, given to the god of eloquence by the god of harmony, is yet, under the name of "The Caduceus," the symbol of Peace, Commerce, and Reconciliation.

HEATH (*Erica vulgaris*).—SOLITUDE.

WHERE can Solitude most surely be found? Where can we betake ourselves so as to be most completely abstracted from surrounding objects? Whither can we bend our steps that we may be the least liable to intrusion from our fellowmen? The answer which may first spring up in the mind will be, perhaps,—In the wilds of nature, on the vast surface of moorland, covered with heather, where not a tree or shrub larger than gorse or furze intercepts the boundless view. Thither, indeed, he who has toiled among and for his kind, and in return has received injury and wrong, may fly to

escape the society in which he has found only disappoint-
ment.   Such an one Wordsworth has portrayed,—

> " He was one who owned
> No common soul.   In youth by science nursed,
> And led by Nature into a wild scene
> Of lofty hopes, he to the world went forth
> A favoured being, knowing no desire
> Which genius did not hallow,—'gainst the taint
> Of dissolute tongues, and jealousy and hate,
> And scorn,—against all enemies prepared,
> All but neglect.   The world, for so it thought,
> Owed him no service : wherefore he at once
> With indignation turned himself away,
> And with the food of pride sustained his soul
> In Solitude.   Stranger ! these gloomy boughs
> Had charms for him ; and here he loved to sit,
>   *   *   *   *   *   *
> And on these barren rocks, with juniper,
> And Heath, and thistle, thinly sprinkled o'er,
> Fixing his downcast eye, he many an hour
> A morbid pleasure nourished, tracing here
> An emblem of his own unfruitful life ;
>   *   *   *   *   *   *
>   *   *   *   and so, lost man !
> On visionary views would fancy feed,
> Till his eye streamed with tears."

To him the barren Heath was solitude indeed ; but not less
may it be found in the crowded streets, thronged with myriads.
of human beings, bent each one upon his pursuit after pleasure or business, seeking how he may carry out his plans for
self or others : there we may pass along undisturbed, our
thoughts concentrated upon the subject of our reflections,

even more fully than when amid the wilds but beauties of nature we wander far away from the busy haunts of our kind ; yet, as an emblem of Solitude, we cannot but regard the Heath as perhaps the most appropriate flower.

HENBANE (*Hyoscyamus niger*).—FAULT.

HENBANE is a medicinal plant of frequent use by living physicians. It is a virulent poison, but in their hands is productive of great benefit in many cases. The Turks are said to make use of it as a narcotic, its effects resembling those of opium, and they who commonly make use of it are regarded as dissolute debauchees.

HEPATICA (*Hepatica triloba*).—CONFIDENCE.

THIS is a great favourite in the flower border, not only on account of the various colours it displays, but their many shades. The leaves are so formed as to bear a striking resemblance to the lobes of the liver, whence its generic name. It blooms from February to April ; and when it spreads forth its pretty petals, the gardener knows that the earth is in a genial state, and that he may with Confidence sow his seeds.

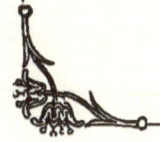

HERB ARCHANGEL (*Angelica Archangelica*).— INSPIRATION.

THE stalks of this culinary plant possess a warm aromatic flavour, and are deemed little inferior to ginger as a stimulant. In Norway and Lapland it is highly esteemed. It is supposed to be indigenous to extreme northern countries, and we are told that it serves to form the wreath for the poets of Lapland, who become inspired under the influence of its agreeable odour.

HOLLY (*Ilex aquifolium*).—FORETHOUGHT.

THE forethought of Nature is shown in a remarkable manner in this beautiful tree. The holly-trees in the forest of Needwood supply ample proof of this, though many more can be found. They are furnished with a belt of leaves armed with thorns to the height of ten feet or more. At that height the leaves cease to be any protection, for above they are smooth at the edges. The tree has no further need to be armed against enemies which cannot reach so high. This tree, which is of the brightest green colour, is the last decoration of our forests when despoiled of their verdure by winter; its berries are food for the little birds which abide with us during that inclement season; it lends them its foliage, which is a hospitable roof prepared for them then. The deer and the hart even seek its shelter; there they conceal themselves behind the snows accumulated around it. The leaves and branches, lightly covered with snow, are disposed like the roof of a Chinese pavilion, the elegant and pyramidal form of which is assumed by the Holly.

Does it not seem, then, that Nature, by a kind foresight, has taken care to preserve throughout the year the greenness of this beautiful tree, to arm it with thorns, suited to the needs of, and for a defence for, innocent creatures which fly to it for refuge ? Southey has well spoken of the peculiarity in the foliation of the Holly, asking,—

" Oh reader! hast thou ever stood to see the Holly Tree ?
The eye that contemplates it well perceives its glossy leaves,
 Ordered by an Intelligence so wise,
 As might confound the Atheist's sophistries.

" Below, a circling fence, its leaves are seen wrinkled and keen ;
No grazing cattle through their prickly round can reach to wound;
 But, as they grow where nothing is to fear,
 Smooth and unarmed the pointless leaves appear."

HOLLYHOCK (*Althæa rosea*).—FRUITFULNESS.

THIS beautiful biennial is universally known and admired. It is a native of China, though some regard it as imported from Syria during the Crusades. This species is the parent of nearly twenty varieties, the colours of which are usually perpetuated in the offspring. Its flowers are very abundant, and the seeds are also numerous, whence it seems to have been most aptly chosen as the emblem of Fruitfulness. The Chinese are said to represent Nature as crowned with its flowers.

THE HONEYSUCKLE (*Caprifolium Periclymenum*).— BONDS OF LOVE.

RECOLLECTIONS of childhood are chiefly associated with pleasurable incidents : hence the scenes mid which our golden age was passed are ever bound round our heart by the fondest regard. Wander where we will over the wide world, form as many new ties as we may, ties the nearest and dearest that the human heart can conceive of, pass through periods of the richest enjoyment that our being is capable of feeling, there is still—latent it may be in general—but there is still a deep, strong, and abiding affection for that particular spot of our native land where our early years were spent. All writers have expressed this, some poets in language the most expressive, as, for instance, Scott :

> " Breathes there the man, with soul so dead,
> Who never to himself hath said,
> This is my own, my native land ! "

and here we have the same feeling shown in more humble lines with which our flower is woven :

> " There the wild Honeysuckle, gaily drest
> In blending hues of yellow and of red,
>   With rich abundance, throws its slender stems
> In beautiful festoons, while its flowers shed
> Their fragrant sweets upon the evening air.
> No blooming shrub's more plentiful or fair,
>   Than Woodbine wild among thy floral gems."

Those Bonds of Love are, perhaps, the last to be broken which bind the child to the parent, especially to the mother. With

her are passed the greater number of hours in infancy and childhood : in that time, under her influence and teaching, our character is formed,—some escape the effects of an injudicious mother's treatment ; others throw off for a time the salutary control of a wise and good mother's teaching,—but the ties of love are not broken ; they remain strong as ever though relaxed. Wordsworth writes of Emily, in " The White Doe of Rylstone :

> " Ere she hath reached yon rustic shed,
> Hung with late-flowering Woodbine, spread
> Along the walls and overhead,
> The fragrance of the breathing flowers
> Revives a memory of those hours
> When here, in this remote alcove,
> A fondly anxious mother strove
> To teach her salutary fears
> And mysteries above her years."

There are Bonds of Love, so called, which produce injurious effects to the young maiden. Mrs. Laurence, addressing Cupid, says :

> " Cruel boy !
> Woodbine all untwined,
> Wanders here forlorn and free ;
> Emblem of the maiden's mind,
> Who has placed her trust in thee."

and for young men, they often work most disastrously. Hear Cowper :

> " So Love, that clings around the noblest minds,
> Forbids th' advancement of the soul he binds ;

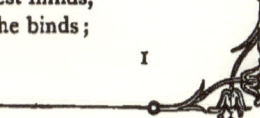

> Then farewell promises of happier fruits,
> Manly designs, and learning's grave pursuits.
>
>   *   *   *   *   *
>
> Who will, may pant for glory and excel."

But the Bonds of Love, which have their origin in esteem for the highest form of mental endowments and moral worth, are pure and holy, beneficial in time and beyond it ; and to these Bonds, Miss Twamley seems to refer, when she says :

> " The Honeysuckle give to Kate, so kindly and caressing ;
> Whoever wins her for a mate, will win both wealth and blessing."

THE HOP (*Humulus Lupulus*).—INJUSTICE.

THE Hop-gardens of England present a beautiful appearance when the flowers are ready to be gathered, and are, perhaps, still more pleasing at the time of "hop-picking," when the scene is animated by the presence of men, women, and children, engaged in the operation. The specific name *Lupulus* is said to be a contraction of Lupulus Salictarius, by which name Pliny says it was known, since growing among willows it twined around them, and was as destructive to them as a wolf to a flock of sheep ; hence it appropriately represents Injustice.

THE HORSE-CHESTNUT (*Æsculus Hippocastanum*).— LUXURY.

NEARLY two centuries and a half have passed since this tree was imported from India, but as yet it does not mingle its gorgeous head with the trees of our forests. It beautifies parks, decorates castles, and lends its shade to our colleges and palaces. In the early spring we see its branches studded with huge leaf-buds, smeared as it were with an unctuous gum ; a showery day comes, producing a warm moist atmosphere ; then the leaf-buds open and clothe the tree with verdure. When standing alone, nothing can exceed the beauty of its foliage and the richness of its flowers. Its pyramidal form, clad with digitate leaves, and the mass of spikes of delicate white and pink flowers, which appear in thick profusion, render it an admirable object ; as Howitt writes :

> " For in its honour prodigal nature weaves
>   A princely vestment, and profusely showers
> O'er its green masses of broad palmy leaves,
>   Ten thousand waxen pyramidal flowers ;
> And gay and gracefully its head it heaves
>   Into the air, and monarch-like it towers."

The wood and fruit of the Horse-chestnut are of little value. Its magnitude confines it to the use of the wealthy as an ornament. It seems thus fitly to represent Luxury in our floral language.

THE HYACINTH (*Hyacinthus orientalis*).—GAME. PLAY.

APOLLO and Hyacinthus are related to have been engaged in playing quoits on the river Amphysus, when a quoit, which had just been hurled from the hand of Apollo, diverged from its intended course and slew the luckless Hyacinthus. The god had not the power to restore his friend to life, but changed him into the beautiful flower which has ever since borne his name. Milton has recorded the incident as follows :

> " Apollo, with unwitting hand,
> Whilome did slay his dearly-loved mate,
> Young Hyacinth, the pride of Spartan land ;
> But then transformed him to a purple flower."

THE HYDRANGEA (*Hydrangea hortensis*).— YOU ARE COLD.

THIS plant was brought from China about eighty years ago. It is highly valued for its great profusion of elegant flowers, which are by nature of a rosy tinge. By culture, under some circumstances, they become blue, an effect which florists seem to aim at. The plant is very ornamental in large rooms and halls; and when the flowers are blue the whole plant has a cold appearance, whence it has been thought to be emblematic of a coquette, who, devoid of any estimable qualities, seeks to please only by attention to her toilet.

THE ICE PLANT (*Mesembryanthemum crystallinum*).—
YOUR LOOKS FREEZE ME.

THIS singular plant is much admired. It needs the warm atmosphere of a hothouse, except in summer, when it flourishes in the open air. The leaves are covered with transparent vesicles filled with water. When the plant is in the shade, it has the appearance of being sprinkled with dew; when exposed to a burning sun, it seems to be heavy with icy crystals, which give it great brilliancy. On these accounts it has received the popular name of Ice Plant. Cowper, alluding to it, says,—

> "the spangled beau,
> Ficoides, glitters bright the winter long."

THE IRIS.—MESSAGE.

MILTON speaks of "Iris all hues," on which account this plant received its name at a very remote period. These colours are very brilliant, and are as various as the colours and shades of the rainbow. Iris has ever been the bearer of good tidings to mortals. When Priam mourned the death of Hector, and longed sore to ransom his body, dragged about by the relentless Achilles, she was sent by Zeus to the heart-broken old man to say,—

> "Fear nothing, Priam, son of Dardanus,
> Nor let thy mind be troubled; not for ill,

But here on kindly errand am I sent :
To thee I come a messenger from Jove,
Who from on high looks down on thee with eyes
Of pitying love ; he bids thee ransom home
The godlike Hector's corpse ; and with thee take
Such presents as may melt Achilles' heart.

(Homer, LORD DERBY'S *Trans.)*

and straightway he does her bidding with success.

IVY *(Hedera helix).*—FRIENDSHIP.

" Friendship, peculiar boon of heaven,
The noble mind's delight and pride,
To men and angels only given,
To all the lower world denied."

FRIENDSHIP is represented by a device in which Ivy is growing round a fallen tree, with the motto, " Nothing can detach me from it." In Greece the hymeneal altar was hung with Ivy, and a branch was presented to a newly-wedded husband, symbolizing the indissoluble union he had just formed. " Nothing," says a popular writer, " can separate the Ivy from the tree which it once embraces; it adorns it with its foliage in the harsh season when its branches bear only the hoar-frost ; the companion of its destinies, it falls when the tree is overthrown ; death even does not work separation, and it decorates with its perpetual verdure the withered trunk of its past supporter," These words are true. The Ivy is held to the soil by its own roots, and derives nothing from the substance of the tree which it embraces. The protector of ruins, it is the ornament of the old walls which support it ; it receives nothing beyond ; but, a constant friend, it dies where it attaches itself.

> " The Ivy, that staunchest and firmest friend,
>   That hastens its succouring arm to lend
>   To the ruined fane, where in youth it sprung,
>   And its pliant tendrils in sport were flung.
>   When the sinking buttress and mouldering tower
>   Seem only the spectres of former power,
>   Then the Ivy clusters around the wall,
>   And for tapestry hangs in the moss-grown hall,
>   Striving in beauty and youth to dress
>   The desolate place in its loneliness."—TWAMLEY.

INDIAN JASMINE (*Bignonia radicans*).—SEPARATION.

How wonderful the harmony which we observe on all sides from the relative adaptation of animal and vegetable life. The butterfly adorns the rose; the nightingale lends her sweet notes to our groves; the bee, in the act of pilfering them, gives animation to the flowers which yield their rich treasure. Thus, throughout nature, the insect is fitted for the flower, the bird for the tree, the quadruped to the plant. Man alone can enjoy the harmony of things, and he alone can break the unison and mutual dependence which exists in the universe. His greedy and rash hand snatches an animal from the climate suited to its being, and thinking only of his own gratification, he too often forgets the plant which would have made his new slave unmindful of the sweetness of its native country. If he brings the plant, he neglects the insect which resorts to it, the bird which enlivens it, the quadruped which feeds upon its foliage and reposes under its shade. Mark, for instance, the Jasmine of Virginia, with its beautiful verdure and purple flowers. It still remains a stranger amongst us. We always prefer to it our lovely honeysuckle, from which bees delight to sip the honey, off which the goat browses its foliage, and which supplies its fruit to myriads of blackbirds, warblers, chaffinches and goldfinches. We do not doubt but that the rich Virginian Jasmine would equal these attractions in our eyes if we could see it enlivened by the humming-bird of Florida, which, in the vast forests of the new world, makes choice of its beautiful foliage in preference to all other shelter. It builds its nest in one of the leaves, which it rolls up like a trumpet; it finds its food in its red flowers, which resemble in shape those of the foxglove, whose nectareous glands it sips from; it conceals within them its little body, when the appearance is as of an emerald set in coral, and it sometimes goes in so far as to allow of its being caught. This little bird is the life and the soul, the perfection of the flower which cherishes it; separated from its aërial guest, this elegant twiner is like a desolate widow who has lost all her charms.

THE JONQUIL (*Narcissus jonquilla*).—DESIRE.

THOMSON writes of "Jonquils of potent fragrance," a quality which several poets have noted. Thus Prior,—

> " The smelling tuberose and Jonquil declare
> The stronger impulse of the evening air,"

and Shenstone,—

> "A various wreath of odorous flowers she made,
> Gay motleyed pinks and sweet Jonquils; she chose
> The violet blue, that on the moss-bank grows;
> All sweet to sense."

In " Flora Domestica," also, this is alluded to,—

> " Gallant Jonquils, fair tuberoses,
> Short is your sweet life ;"

and the American poet Bidlake says,—

> " The Jonquil loads with potent breath the air,
> And rich in golden glory nods."

Its strong fragrance, at first agreeable, soon becomes oppressive ; it is a pretty flower, and by the Turks has been made the emblem of Desire.

JUNIPER *(Juniperus communis).*—ASYLUM. SUCCOUR.

" Sweet is the Juniper, but sharp his bough."—SPENSER.

THE ancients consecrated this shrub to the Eumenides ; the smoke of its burning green branches was the incense which they offered to the deities of the lower regions ; they used to burn its berries at funerals, to ward off malevolent spirits. The simple peasantry now think that the perfume of the Juniper berry purifies the air, and protects their humble dwelling from evil genii.

This shrub is sometimes grown in gardens, but it does not yield kindly to cultivation. In its wild state it delights in the borders of forests. Weak and timid creatures seek an asylum under its long branches, which cover the earth around. The hare in her extremity squats with confidence beneath it, for its strong odour puts her canine pursuers at fault; the thrush builds in it a house for her young, and feeds upon its fruit; the entomologist finds among its twigs, bristling with thorns, numerous shining insects, which have no other shelter, and which seem to divine that this shrub is destined to be their refuge.

LANTANA (*L. Cammara*).—SHARPNESS.

THE Cammara is a native of the West Indies. It is a small bushy plant, with flowers white as snow, and varying, as pink, yellow, and orange. It is of a peculiar aromatic odour, but its twigs and branches are so beset with thorns, that if we bring the hand into contact with them we are instantly sensible of their Sharpness.

LARCH (*Larix communis*).—BOLDNESS.

THE Larch loves to grow upon lofty mountains, where it rises from thirty to eighty feet. Hence it is a fit emblem of Boldness, as well also because it seems to thrive where scarce any other tree will grow, and it clothes with soil the almost bare rocks of our hill-sides in a few years. It is an invaluable; tree and as we have passed over different barren and bleak wastes of England, we have oft been surprised that the owners have not made use of this tree, both to ameliorate the climate, and clothe the surface with an artificial covering of earth.

THE LARKSPUR (*Delphinium consolida*).—SWIFTNESS.

THE calyx in this pretty field flower is divided into five oblong segments, with a long spur at the base, either straight or curved, whence its name. This species is called *Pied-d'Alouette* by the French. The whole genus are popular border flowers, perennial, and needing little or no care in cultivation.

THE LAUREL (*Laurus nobilis*).—GLORY.

" GLORY claims the Bay," as its emblem, says Miss Twamley, and of its leaves has the wreath of victory, both in games and war, been formed. The warrior,—

> "his crown of laurel-leaves
> With bloody hand when victor weaves."—SCOTT.

and Percival tells us that

> " Fame's bright star and glory's swell
> By the glossy leaf of the Bay are given ;"

though no one needs reminding of this who has read or heard aught of the history of ancient Greece or Rome. In the latter city, for ordinary uses at the temple, and for wreathing the altars, the laurel was obtained near the fountain of Castalia ; but on rare and very important occasions the citizens sent to Tempe for their Laurel.

The Sweet-Bay has also been used for wreaths to crown philosophers, and orators, and poets ; and Herrick wished that a Laurel tree might be planted upon his grave. He writes,—

> " A funeral stone or verse, I covet none;
> But only crave of you that I may have
> A sacred Laurel springing from my grave ;
> Which being seen blest with perpetual greene,
> May grow to be not so much called a tree,
> As the eternal monument of me."

LAURESTINUS (*Viburnum tinus*).—I DIE IF NEGLECTED.

THIS native of the South of Europe is one of our prettiest and most popular evergreen shrubs. It is highly ornamental to our groves and shrubberies, displaying its small white flowers at a season when all other shrubs have shed theirs.

Neither the scorching breath of summer, nor the cold north wind of winter, robs this shrub of its charms. Still, to preserve it, it needs care, and there are now and then winters so severe that the frost will destroy its vitality down to the ground. The emblem of constant and gentle friendship, we should say it always desires to please, but it dies if neglected.

LAVENDER (*Lavandula spica*).—DISTRUST.

A NOTION prevailed in days of yore that the Asp, a most dangerous kind of viper, delighted chiefly to dwell under the Lavender plant; which on that account was always approached with Distrust.

It yields an agreeable scent by distillation, and its dried stems and leaves and flowers supply a most pleasing means of perfuming many domestic articles. Miss Strickland says its "fragrance never dies." Shenstone writes,—

> " And Lavender, whose spikes of azure bloom
> Shall be, erewhile, in arid bundles bound,
> To lurk amidst the labours of her loom,
> And crown her kerchiefs clean with mickle rare perfume."

LETTUCE (*Lactuca sativa*).—COLDNESS.

THIS well-known garden plant is the suitable emblem of Coldness, but of Coldness most agreeable, since nothing is more delicious to the palate than the crisp, juicy heart of the Lettuce in the hot days of summer.

LILAC (*Syringa vulgaris*).—FIRST EMOTION OF LOVE.

THE Lilac has been made the emblem of the first Emotion of Love, because nothing has greater charms than this pleasing shrub on the return of Spring. The freshness of its verdure, the flexibility of its branches, the abundance of its flowers, their beauty so brief and transient, their colour so soft and varied, all remind us of those delightful emotions, which add charms to beauty and impart to youth a divine gracefulness.

The Lilac, for aught we can see in it, seems to have been formed simply to gratify the sense of sight and smell! What a combination of fragrance, freshness, grace, and delicacy is it! what variety in detail, what beauty as a whole!

> " The Lilac various in array, now white,
> Now sanguine, and her beauteous head now set
> With purple spikes pyramidal, as if
> Studious of ornament, yet unresolved
> Which hue she most approved, she chose them all."
>
> COWPER.

Two American poets speak the most decidedly of its perfume. Willis says,—

> "The Lilac has a load of balm
> For every wind that stirs ;"

and Longfellow,—

> " How slowly through the lilac-scented air
> Descends the tranquil moon !"

THE LILY (*Lilium candidum*).—MAJESTY.

" The Lily's height bespoke command,
    A fair imperial flower ;
She seemed designed for Flora's hand,
    The sceptre of her power."—COWPER.

FROM the middle of a tuft of long leaves, which in unfolding
themselves fall back one upon another, so as to form a round
green couch, there rises an elegant and stately stem, which
is terminated by a cluster of long buds of a soft and shining
green. Time imperceptibly swells and blanches the buds of
this pretty bunch, and, towards the middle of June, they
bend downwards and unfold in six petals of sparkling whiteness. Their union forms those admirable vases, in which
nature delights to set golden stamens, from which gush forth
wavelets of perfume. These beautiful flowers, half-inclined
around the lofty stem, seem to exact and receive the homage
of nature ; but yet the Lily, notwithstanding her charms, needs
a court in order to appear in her full lustre. Alone, she is
cold and as one forsaken ; surrounded by many other flowers,
she throws them all into the shade. She is a sovereign ; her
charm is the charm of Majesty :

" The fair Lily's bell was set
    With a bright dewy coronet."—MISS BROWNE.

The Lily has ever been regarded also as the emblem of
whiteness, and hence of purity. So long ago as when the
apocryphal books of the Old Testament were written, no
title could better distinguish the Jewish matron whose spot-

less chastity is there recorded, than Susannah, the White Lily.

LILY OF THE VALLEY (*Convallaria majalis*).—
RETURN OF HAPPINESS.

"Fair flower, that, lapt in lowly glade, dost hide beneath the greenwood shade,
  Than whom the vernal gale
None fairer wakes, on bank or spray, our England's Lily of the May,
  Our Lily of the vale !"—BISHOP MANT.

THIS greatly admired flower loves the recesses of our valleys, the shade of oak-trees, and the banks of flowing streams. From the early days of May she unfolds her ivory flowers, and scatters their fragrance around. Then the nightingale forsakes our hedges and our thickets, and seeks in the forest glade a companion, a loneliness and an echo which responds to his song; led by the perfume of the Lily of the Valley, the lovely bird soon finds an agreeable asylum ; there he takes up his abode, where he celebrates, in most melodious notes, solitude and love, and the flower which, in each succeeding Spring, proclaims to him the Return of Happiness.

Shelley calls our flower a Naiad,—

" The Naiad-like Lily of the Vale,
Whom youth makes so fair and passion so pale,
That the light of its tremulous bells is seen
Through their pavilions of tender green ;"

128

Wordsworth speaks of " that shy plant,"—

> " The Lily of the Vale,
> That loves the ground, and from the sun withholds
> Her pensive beauty ; from the breeze her sweets ; "

and Thomson bids us " seek the bank,"—

> " Where, scattered wide, the Lily of the Vale
> Her balmy essence breathes."

Wiffen thus expresses his admiration of the Lily of the Valley,—

> " Her flower, the vestal nun who (lone) abideth ;
> Her breath, that of celestials meekly wooed
> From heaven ; her leaf, the holy veil which hideth
> Her from the shrine where purity resideth ;
> Spring's darling, nature's pride, the sylvan's queen."

Who does not promptly join in this? What flowers do we look for so frequently, so eagerly, as for those of the Lily of the Valley which attend, if they do not foretell, the return of the happy days of Spring and Summer, which follow the dreariness and gloom of winter?

THE LIME TREE (*Tilia rubra*).—CONJUGAL LOVE.

> " A murmur of the bee
> Dwells ever in the honeyed Lime."—MRS. HEMANS.

ZEUS and Hermes, in human form, visited Phrygia. They were refused hospitality by all until they came to the dwelling of Philemon and Baucis, who entertained them kindly. Zeus compensated them by taking them to a lofty eminence, and preserving them from a flood which covered the low-land. There also was a temple of Zeus, of which he made his hosts the guardians. He allowed them to die at the same moment, and changed them into trees, Baucis into a Lime, as supposed, and Philemon into an Oak, hence the Lime is the emblem of Conjugal Love.

Beauty, grace, simplicity, extreme gentleness, have ever been regarded as indispensable qualities in a loving wife. All these we may find symbolized in the Linden Tree. Every Spring it clothes itself with foliage of a pale green. Its flowers are very odoriferous, and supply an abundance of honey to the bee, which is always buzzing amongst its branches. An infusion of its flowers is deemed a most valuable beverage in some cases of sickness. Its wood is turned into bowls, dishes, and doctor's boxes. Its twigs make baskets and cradles. Its bark furnished writing tablets. Shoemakers use it for cutting leather upon. The most elegant use to which it is applied is wood-carving. St. Paul's Cathedral; Chatsworth; Trinity College, Cambridge; and many other famous structures are ornamented by its means. Its services are so great that it well represents the good wife, whose hand is ever busy, and whose mind is capable of directing it, so as to render home happy.

LUCERN (*Medicago sativa*).—LIFE.

LUCERN grows in the same spot for a long time, but when it leaves it, it is for ever. On this account it has been made the emblem of life. Nothing is more pleasing to the eye than a field of Lucern in bloom, which resembles a green carpet variegated with violet. Where sown it yields abundant crops, without demanding care. Mown down, it springs again freely. The young heifer rejoices to see it. Sheep are fond of it. It is a delicacy for deer, and horses delight in it. Indigenous to our land, it is a gift direct from heaven. We own it without an effort, we enjoy it without observation or acknowledgment. We often prefer a flower of fleeting charms to this useful plant, just as we abandon, too frequently, a certain good to run after empty pleasures which take wing and flee away.

MADDER (*Rubia tinctorum*).—CALUMNY.

THIS plant is well known as yielding a red and scarlet dye for clothiers and calico-printers. It is for the most part imported from Holland, though at one time it was cultivated here under difficulties. Sheep and animals feeding upon it have their milk and bones dyed by it ; and when they feed alternately upon this and grass, the bones are dyed in concentric circles. Sheep's teeth, when eating it, are tinged as with the blood of a victim, which imputes a sanguinary disposition to an animal the most simple ; thus malice will sometimes profit by a false appearance to calumniate innocence itself.

MADWORT (*Alyssum saxatile*).—TRANQUILLITY.

A VERY ornamental plant early in the season. It was thought by the ancients to possess the property of allaying anger, and consequently of producing Tranquillity. Some persons still entertain the notion that it has that valuable quality.

MANCHINEEL (*Hippomane Mancinella*).—DUPLICITY.

THE fruit of the Manchineel has a pleasing appearance and an agreeable fragrance, which tempt one to eat it. Its spongy and flabby substance, however, contains a milky and treacherous juice, which is at first unsavoury, but is quickly perceived to be so highly caustic as to burn at once the lips, the palate, and the tongue. It is thus a fit emblem of Duplicity.

MAIDENHAIR (*Adiantum Capillus-veneris*).— DISCRETION.

PLINY says that it is to no purpose that you plunge the Adiantum into water, for it always remains dry. Even so we are told does this pretty fern conceal from botanists the secret processes in its flowering and seeding. It intrusts to Zephyrus alone the invisible germs of its offspring. That god makes choice of their birthplace and nursery. Sometimes he is pleased to make their wavy hair the veil which screens from observation the cave, in which the solitary naïad sleeps from the earliest period; at others he bears them upon his wings and makes them radiant stars of green in the turrets of an ancient castle, or else arranges them as light festoons, and decorates with them the cool resorts and loved shades of shepherds. Thus this fern puts science at fault, and hides her secret origin from eyes the most penetrating; while she hastens to reward by her beauty the hand that nurses her.

THE MANDRAKE (*Mandragora officinalis*).—RARITY.

THE ancients attributed remarkable virtues to the Mandrake; but as they have not left any accurate description of the plant, we do not know to what species they gave the name. Mountebanks who are able to make a profit out of popular errors, know how to give the appearance of a little man to the roots of bryony and other plants, which, they assure the credulous, are genuine roots of the Mandrake. They allege that they are only found in a small canton of China, which is almost inaccessible. They assert that these Mandrakes utter the most lamentable cries when torn up by the roots, a statement made use of by Longfellow, where he says,—

"teach me where that wondrous Mandrake grows,
Whose magic root, torn from the earth with groans,
At midnight hour, can scare the fiends away,
And make the mind prolific in its fancies!"

They further affirm that he who uproots them dies soon after.

A volume might be filled with an account of the fanciful, absurd, and superstitious ideas, which have produced many old errors as to the opposite virtues of a plant which, perhaps, never existed.

MARIGOLD (*Calendula officinalis*).—PAIN. CHAGRIN.

ALL the world knows this golden-coloured flower, which symbolizes mental sorrow, as when Phœbus

> "down declines, she droops and mourns,
> Bedewed as 'twere with tears, till he returns ;
> And * * veils her flowers when he is gone
> As if she——
> ——did contemn (despise)
> To wait upon a meaner light than him."—WITHERS.

This flower offers to the observer many remarkable singularities. It blooms the whole year, or during the *calends* of each month, whence its name Calendula. Its flowers are open from 9 A.M. to 3 P.M. only ; yet they always turn to the sun, and follow him in his course from east to west.

The sorrowful signs of the Marigold may be modified in many ways. Joined with roses, it is the emblem of the sweet sorrows of love ; alone, it expresses ennui ; woven with different flowers it represents the ever-varying course of life, a mixture of good and ill ; in the East, a bouquet of

Marigolds and Poppies says, " I will soothe your grief." It is especially by the like modifications that the Language of Flowers becomes the interpreter of our sentiments.

MARYGOLD AND CYPRESS.—Despair.

CYPRESS is the emblem of Death; the Marygold of Chagrin and Pain ; together, the two plants are the emblem of Despair.

MARSH MALLOW (*Althæa officinalis*).—Beneficence.

EMBLEM of Beneficence, the Marsh Mallow is the friend of the poor. It grows naturally by the stream which quenches their thirst, and near the cottages which they dwell in ; but it yields to cultivation, and we sometimes see its unassuming stalks mingling with our garden flowers. It is free from bitterness, and its appearance is agreeable ; its flesh-coloured flowers harmonize with its leaves and stems, and the whole plant is covered with a silken silvery down. It is pleasant alike to the eye, and to the hand which touches it. Its flowers, stems, leaves, and roots, are equally useful. Syrups and lozenges are made with its juices, and are as agreeable to the palate, as they are beneficial to health. The traveller in his wanderings sometimes finds the root a healthy and sub-stantial food. We need only to look about our feet to find all nature full of love and foresight ; but this gentle mother has often hidden, in plants as well as in man, the greatest virtues under the most unpretending aspect.

MARVEL OF PERU (*Mirabilis Jalapa*).—TIMIDITY.

THIS is one of the most fragrant of flowers. It is highly ornamental. In a state of cultivation it sports into many varieties. Our continental neighbours call it Belle-de-nuit, because its flowers spread their beauty to the night. Hence it is regarded as the emblem of Timidity,—here are the first four lines of an address to this flower by Constant Dubois, referring to its supposed timidity in shunning the brilliancy of day, and preferring the subdued light of evening.

> " Solitaire amante des nuits,
> Pourquoi ces timides alarmes,
> Quand ma muse au jour que tu fuis
> S'apprête à révéler tes charmes ? "

MEADOW ANEMONE (*Anemone pratensis*).—SICKNESS.

THE inhabitants of some districts are of opinion that this ornamental field flower exhales from its dark purple blossom a pernicious odour, which so poisons the air that they who breathe it are subject to the most frightful maladies.

MEADOW SAFFRON (*Colchicum autumnale*).—MY BEST DAYS ARE PAST.

TOWARDS the last days of summer there may be seen, shining upon the green sward of moist meadows, a flower like the Spring Crocus. That flower is the Autumnal Crocus. Far from inspiring us with joy and hope, as the former does, this proclaims the departure of the bright days of summer.

This plant was supposed to be indigenous in the fields of Colchis, and was mythically alleged to have sprung from some drops of the fluid which Medea prepared to restore the aged Æson to youth. This fabulous origin has led to the popular belief that Meadow Saffron is a preservative against all kinds of sickness. The Swiss attach it to the neck of their infants, as a charm against every evil.

Meadow Saffron possesses great attractions for the scientific naturalist in its singular botanical phenomena. Its corolla, of which there are six divisions, of a pale violet purple, has neither leaves nor stem. A long tube, nearly as white as ivory, which is nothing but the prolongation of the flower, is its only support. At the bottom of this tube nature has deposited the seed, which ripens only in the following Spring. Its inclosing sheath, buried deep under the grass, braves the perils of winter : and in the beautiful days of the young year, this species of cradle rises up from the soil, and submits itself to the sun's rays, surrounded by a tuft of large green leaves. Thus this plant, reversing the common effect of the seasons, mingles its fruit with the flowers of Spring, and its flowers with the fruits of Autumn. If ever Melancholy weaves a garland of its pale bluish flowers, it dedicates it to happy days which have fled never more to return.

MEADOW SWEET (*Spiræa Ulmaria*).—USELESSNESS.

THIS herbaceous plant, which is also called in France the Queen of the Meadows, has been designated a useless beauty, because the chemist and the physician have failed to detect any valuable property in it ; and because animals do not feed upon it. It is very fragrant, very pretty, and is always a pleasing object in the latter part of Summer in our moist meadows, and by the side of ponds and pools.

MICHAELMAS DAISY (*Aster Tradescanti*).—AFTER-THOUGHT.

> " We'll pass by the garden that leads to the gate,
> But where is its gaiety now ?
> The Michaelmas Daisy blows lonely and late,
> And the yellow leaf whirls from the bough."—TAYLOR.

THE Michaelmas Daisy begins to display her bloom, when all other flowers are becoming rare. It is as an After-thought of Flora, who bestows upon us a parting smile on her quitting our parterres.

MIGNONETTE (*Reseda odorata*).—YOUR QUALITIES SURPASS YOUR CHARMS.

> " Mignonette's meek humble form,
> Without one tint upon her modest garb
> To draw the idle stare of wandering eyes,
> *   *   *   *   * rich
> In precious fragrance is that lowly one,
> So loved for her sweet qualities, that I
> Should woo her first amid a world of flowers."—TWAMLEY.

A LITTLE more than a century ago the Mignonette was brought to us from Egypt. Linnæus could think of nothing inferior to the divine ambrosia wherewith he could compare it. The perfume is most delicious and of the greatest strength at sunrise and sunset. It blooms from earliest Spring to latest Autumn, in the border or the window garden. Its blooming may be delayed till winter; it may even be converted into a ligneous plant, by careful means, so as to form a small shrub, and live for years.

Mignonette has nothing in its appearance to attract our notice, but its perfume makes it a universal favourite; thus it has become the emblem of one who, without pretension to beauty, possesses qualities which command profound respect and affection, and constrain us to say, " Your qualities surpass your charms."

MILKWORT (*Polygala vulgaris*).—HERMITAGE.

THIS plant, with pretty blue flowers, is always covered with foliage similar to the leaves of Box. Hermits, who formerly loved to dwell in elevated localities, planted it about their abodes. The ancients thought it good food for cattle, and that it increased the quantity of their milk. It is full of a milky juice, whence its name, which signifies *much milk.*

MISTLETOE (*Viscum album*).—I RISE ABOVE ALL.

" Oaks, from whose branches
Garlands of Spanish moss and of mystic Mistletoe flaunted,
Such as the Druids cut down with golden hatchets at Yule-tide."—
LONGFELLOW.

THE Mistletoe is a small shrub which grows on the top of large trees. The grand oak is its slave, and nourishes it with its substance. The Druids had a sort of adoration for a weakness so superior to strength. This master of the oak appeared to them to be equally formidable to men and to gods. Balder, son of the goddess Friga, was invulnerable through her powerful conjurations. His principal enemy, however, discovered that she had overlooked the Mistletoe, and during the fight of the gods, he came to the blind Heder, and desired him to aim at Balder, presenting him with a piece of the plant. Heder hurled the branch, and Balder fell lifeless. Thus was the invulnerable son of a goddess killed by a Mistletoe branch thrown by one blind. Such is said to be the origin of the reverence shown to this shrub by the Gauls.

Longfellow sings of this,

" Balder the Beautiful is dead, is dead.

    *   *   *   *   *

All things in earth and air bound were by magic spell
Never to do him harm ; even the plants and stones ;
All save the Mistletoe, the sacred Mistletoe !

Hæder, the blind old god, whose feet are shod with silence,
Pierced through that gentle breast with his sharp spear, by fraud
Made of the Mistletoe, the accursed Mistletoe !"

MOCK ORANGE (*Philadelphus coronarius*).—FRATERNAL AFFECTION.

ONE of the Ptolemies, Kings of Egypt, made himself worthy of the highest regard by the love he showed for his brother. A kind of syringa has been consecrated to his memory, and his surname Philadelphus, that is to say, Brotherly Love, serves to designate the genus of which there are four species in cultivation.

MOONWORT (*Lunaria biennis*).—FORGETFULNESS.

THIS plant has several names, which have been given to it on account of the broad round silvery silicles, which are moon-shaped. The film which presents this form retains its brilliancy, and has some resemblance to a piece of money, or to a cake called Oublie by the French. It is said that René, Duke of Bar and Lorraine, having been taken prisoner at the battle of Thoulongean, painted by his own hand a branch of Lunaria, and sent it to his people to reproach them for their tardiness in securing his freedom.

MOSS.—MATERNAL LOVE.

LAPLAND mothers are said to wrap their infant offspring in ermine, and cradle them in moss. Nothing can form a softer couch, and when we think of ourselves as wearied in a pedestrian excursion, we fancy that a moss-covered bank, beneath an umbrageous tree, might be the luxury then most desirable. Wordsworth says,

> " There is a fresh and lovely sight,
> A beauteous heap, a hill of moss,
> Just half a foot in height.
> All lovely colours there you see,

All colours that were ever seen ;
And mossy net-work too is there ;
As if by hand of lady fair
The work had woven been ;
And cups, the darlings of the eye,
So deep is their vermilion dye.
Ah me ! what lovely tints are there !
Of olive-green and scarlet bright,
In spikes, and branches, and in stars,
Green, red, and pearly white !"

THE MOSS ROSE (*Rosa muscosa*).—LOVE.
VOLUPTUOUSNESS.

" The angel of the flowers, one day, beneath a Rose-tree sleeping lay ;
Awaking from his light repose, the angel whispered to the Rose,
' O fondest object of my care, still fairest found, where all is fair ;
For the sweet shade thou giv'st to me, ask what thou wilt, 'tis granted
thee !'
' Then,' said the Rose, with deepened glow, ' on me another grace
bestow.'
The spirit paused in silent thought :—What grace was there the flower
had not ?
'Twas but a moment—o'er the Rose a veil of moss the angel throws ;
And robed in nature's simplest weed, could there a flower that Rose
exceed."—*From the German.*

ON seeing the Moss Rose—the rose without a thorn—and
its flower surrounded by a soft and pleasing verdure, one has
said that Voluptuousness wished to dispute with Love for this
beautiful flower. Madame de Genlis says, that, on her return
from England, it was at her house where all Paris went to
see the first rose of this kind. That lady was then cele-

brated, and it is supposed that to see the Moss Rose,
was nothing but a pretext with the crowd to force themselves into her society.

MUGWORT (*Artemisia vulgaris.*)—HAPPINESS.

THIS species of Wormwood is said to be used in some
parts of Sweden in the place of hops, so as to render beer
more stimulating. It was at one time supposed to possess
valuable properties, able to relieve persons suffering from
maladies, the removal of which tended to restore them to
their usual state of health, and thus endow them with as
much of happiness as is allotted to mortals.

MUSHROOM (*Agaricus campestris*).—SUSPICION.

THERE are several species of Mushroom which are a deadly
poison. The Ostiaks of Siberia, make of some of them a
preparation which causes the death of the strongest man in
twelve hours. Many in our climate are also dangerous ; and
there are those which contain a fluid so acrid, that a single
drop put upon the tongue raises a blister. Yet the Russians,
during their long Lent, sustain themselves chiefly on Mush-
rooms, and we ourselves regard the species named at the
head of this article, dressed in various ways, as a choice
delicacy. Nevertheless we cannot safely lay aside Suspicion
in considering the character of those submitted to us, before

making use of them, lest we should unwittingly partake of such as would produce injurious effects, though it might be short of death.

MOSCHATEL (*Adoxa Moschatellina*).—WEAKNESS.

THIS plant, commonly called the Musk Plant, has early in the morning and in the evening a musky odour, which, even to persons who dislike musk, is pleasant. It is general all over Europe, delighting in woods ; but, as its generic name implies, it is without note.

MUSK ROSE (*Rosa moschata*).—CAPRICIOUS BEAUTY.

THE small flowers of this Rose would be wanting in effect but that they grow in panicles. Their fine musky fragrance also renders them pleasing. The plant is, however, very capricious, so to say ; for all at once it droops in situations which at first appeared most favourable. One year it is laden with innumerable bouquets of flowers ; the following it may have no bloom at all.

THE MYROBALAN (*Prunus cerasifera*).—BEREAVEMENT.

THIS tree is like the plum-tree, bearing white flowers in April and May, and offering to us a fruit which resembles in form and colour a very beautiful cherry. This contains nothing but an insipid and disagreeable juice ; so that even birds reject that which we would leave to them.

MYRTLE (*Myrtus communis*).—LOVE.

"The Myrtle bough bids lovers live."—WALTER SCOTT.

THE oak has ever been dedicated to Jupiter; the laurel to
Apollo; the olive to Minerva; and the Myrtle to Venus.
Perpetual verdure, supple branches laden with fragrant
flowers, which seem destined to adorn the brow of Love, has
procured for the Myrtle the honour of being the tree of
Venus. The chief temple of that goddess at Rome was
surrounded by a myrtle grove. In Greece she was worshipped under the name of Myrtea. When she rose from the
foam of the sea she was presented with a wreath of Myrtle.
She was crowned with Myrtle by the Cupids. Being surprised by a band of Satyrs on coming out of her bath, she
took refuge behind a Myrtle bush. It was with a branch of
this tree that she chastised the audacious Psyche, who compared her own fleeting beauty to the immortal loveliness of
the goddess. Subsequently the garland of Love has sometimes decorated the warrior's brow. After the rape of the
Sabines, the Romans crowned themselves with Myrtle in
honour of Venus victrix. The Myrtle crown then shared the
privilege of the Laurel, and shone upon the head of the successful warrior in his triumph.

Though the Triumphs of ancient Rome have passed away,
Roman ladies retain a taste for this pretty shrub. It is said
that they prefer its fragrance to the most precious essences,
and that they mix with their baths water distilled with
its leaves, under the idea that the tree of Venus bestows

additional charms. If the ancients had that notion, if the tree of Venus was with them the tree of love, it was because they observed that the Myrtle, when taking possession of a plot of ground, banished all other plants. Thus Love, when ruler of the heart, leaves no room there for any other feeling.

THE NETTLE (*Urtica urens*).—CRUELTY.

THE puncture of the Nettle causes a burning pain. If we examine the leaves of Urtica urens, we find a number of fine, stiff, jointed, and pointed hairs, which are so many conduits for an acrid and caustic humour, which is contained in a bladder at the bottom of each. The hair and the bladder are like the sting of the bee. Both in that and also in the plant it is the acrid humour which causes the pain.

NIGHT-SMELLING GERANIUM (*Pelargonium triste*).— MELANCHOLY SPIRIT.

THIS charming plant, like those who suffer from melancholy, flies the light of day; but its delicious perfume delights those who cultivate it. Its clothing is dark and simple. It is a striking contrast to the Scarlet Geranium, the emblem of Folly.

THE OAK (*Quercus pedunculata*).—HOSPITALITY.

"A broad Oak, stretching forth its leafy arms
From an adjoining pasture, overhung
Small space of that green churchyard with a light
And pleasant awning. On the moss-grown wall
My ancient friend and I together took
Our seats."   WORDSWORTH.

THE earlier inhabitants of the earth thought that the Oak, created with the earth, supplied to the first of our race both food and shelter. Sacred to Jupiter, this tree gave shade to the cradle of that god, when born in Arcadia, on Mount Lyceum. The crown of oak leaves, less valued by the Greeks than a golden crown, seemed to the Romans the most desirable reward. He who would win it must be a citizen, have slain an enemy, recovered a battle, or saved the life of a Roman. Scipio Africanus refused the civic crown when tendered to him for having saved his father on the field of Trebia, because he deemed the action its own sufficient reward. The Celts worshipped the Oak, regarding it as the emblem of Hospitality, a virtue which they held so dear, that, next to the title of "Hero," the "Friend of the Stranger" was with them the most valued designation.

The Oak is specially deserving of being assigned by us as the emblem of Hospitality, because it furnished a refuge to our King, Charles the Second, on his escape from the field of battle in which his army was routed.

ORANGE FLOWERS (*Citrus Aurantium*).—CHASTITY.

THE fair brow of a virgin bride is wreathed with a garland of Orange blossom, meet emblem of her maiden purity. This decoration is withheld from all who are undeserving of the distinction, more especially in the neighbourhood of Paris.

THE ORANGE TREE.—GENEROSITY.

THIS is a very handsome shrub, of a shining green throughout all seasons, never bare of most odoriferous flowers, and at all times bearing some of its brilliant, fragrant, and delicious fruit. It is the emblem of a generous friend whose countenance is ever radiant with good nature, whose lips cheer us with kindly words, and whose hands are ever open to bestow upon us his favours.

THE PANSY (*Viola tricolor*).—THINK OF ME.

" THERE is Pansies, that's for thoughts," says Shakespeare and Miss Twamley asks,

> " Oh ! are not Pansies emblems meet for thoughts?
> The pure, the chequered—gay and deep by turns ;
> A hue for every mood the bright things wear
> In their soft velvet coats—"

and, as its English name seems to be a corruption of a French word in the phrase, *Pensez-a-moi—think of me*, it is also called Heart's-ease, a sure result of a confident assurance that those whom we love are not unmindful of us when present or absent; not so unmindful, that is, as to be careless and thoughtless of those claims we have upon their regard and affection.

PARSLEY (*Apium Petroselinum*).—FEAST. BANQUET.

PARSLEY was held in great esteem by the Greeks. In their banquets they wreathed their brows with its slender branches, because they thought it had the effect of increasing cheerfulness and their appetite. At Rome, in their games, the victors were crowned with Parsley. It is thought that Sardinia is the native region of this plant, because that province is represented on ancient medals, by a female figure, near which is a vase containing a bunch of parsley; but the plant seems indigenous to all the cool and shady parts of Greece, and even to the southern provinces of France.

The plant is a very pretty garnishing to our dishes, and certainly enlivens the *tout ensemble* of the festive board, and if its presence does not increase cheerfulness, its absence will sometimes produce the opposite effect.

PASQUE-FLOWER ANEMONE (*A. Pulsatilla*).—YOU ARE WITHOUT PRETENSION.

THIS is a plant which is covered with down, and is all over soft and whitish. It blooms continually through the Summer with a quantity of pretty purple flowers. It prefers the shade, where it is highly ornamental to our borders. It demands no care, and abundantly sows itself.

PASSION-FLOWER (*Passiflora cœrulea*).—CHRISTIAN FAITH.

"High o'er the pointal, decked with gold, (emblem mysterious to behold!)
A radiant cross its form expands ;
Its opening arms appear to embrace the whole collective human race,
Refuse of all men, in all lands."—ANON.

A VIVID imagination has traced in this flower figures of a crown of thorns, the scourge, the sponge, the nails, and the five wounds of Christ ; on account of these fancied resemblances it has been called Passiflora, or the Passion-flower.

PATIENCE DOCK (*Rumex Patientia*).—PATIENCE.

MEDICAL science used to avail itself of the roots of this plant, which are extremely bitter. The name is ambiguous. It is used ambiguously by Mademoiselle Scudery, "*La patience n'est pas la fleur des Français.*" Passerat has also written in his *Jardin d'Amour*,

"On peut en ce jardin cueillir la Patience,
De la prendre en amour je n'ai pas la science."

THE PÆONY (*Pæonia officinalis*).—SHAME.

THIS flower has been made emblematical of Shame, because Rapin, in his poem, *Des Jardins*, speaking of the Pæony, says, "They are not the blushes of modesty which

suffuse it with its rosy hues, but the redness which guilt imparts, for this plant is the hiding place of a culpable nymph."

PEPPERMINT (*Mentha piperita*).—WARMTH OF SENTIMENT.

PROSERPINA is said to have discovered a rival, in intrigue with his sable majesty, her husband. The goddess, justly indignant, changed that rival into this plant, which seems to combine in its distinct effects upon the palate the coldness of fear with the warmth of love. We cultivate this plant under the name of Peppermint, and we owe to it the lozenges which bear its name, and also a valuable essence of much use in medicine.

THE PERIWINKLE.—PLEASING REMEMBRANCES.

ALREADY have the winds purified the atmosphere, scattered the seeds of vegetation over the earth and chased away the gloomy clouds; the air is fresh and pure, the sky seems lifted higher above our head, the greenness of the grass is revived on all sides, and the trees are covered with leaf-buds. Nature is about to deck herself with flowers, but first she prepares the back-ground of her pictures; she covers them with a general tint of verdure which is infinite in variety, which rejoices our eyes and fills our hearts with hope. For some time we have found in sheltered spots, the violet, the daisy, the primrose, and the dandelion. Along the skirts of woods the anemone and the periwinkle display a long net-work of verdure and flowers. These two friendly plants exchange and mingle their mutual charms. The anemone, with its soft foliage, deeply cut, is of a pretty green. The periwinkle has its leaves evergreen, firm, and shining. The flower of the periwinkle is blue; that of the anemone pure white, with a rosy or faint purple edging. The anemone lasts but a day, but she reminds us of the vivid pleasures and fleeting joys of our childhood. The periwinkle emblematizes a more lasting happiness; its colour is that which friendship makes choice of, and its flower was to Rousseau, the emblem of Pleasing Remembrances. "I was going," he said, "to reside at Charmettes, with Madame de Warens; while walking, she saw something blue in the hedge, and said to me, ' *Voilà de la pervenche encore en fleur.*'"

[*Pervenche*, a modern French form of the Norman-French name of this flower, as spoken of by Chaucer,

> "There sprang the violet all newe,
> And fresh *pervinke*, rich of hewe."]

"I had never seen the periwinkle," Rousseau adds; "I did not stoop to examine it, and I had too brief a view of it to distinguish plants on the ground as I stood upright. I only cast a glance upon it as I passed, and nearly thirty years had elapsed without my seeing the periwinkle again, or thought of it. In 1764, being at Gressien, with my friend, M. du Peyron, we were going up a little hill, at the top of which was a pretty room, which he justly called Bellevue. I began to botanize a little. While going up higher, and looking round among the bushes, I uttered a cry of joy, '*Oh ! voila de la pervenche !*' And so indeed it was."

This plant, a charming image of earliest affections, attaches itself firmly to the spot which it beautifies; it embraces all around it with its flexible branches; it covers all with its flowers, which seem to reflect the colour of the sky. So with our first fond impressions received from what is deservedly to be loved—impressions so vivid, so pure, so innocent, that they seem to have a heavenly origin. They stamp our life in an instant with happiness, and we are indebted to them for the most delightful reminiscences. The authors of "Bouquet des Souvenirs" make the flowers themselves affirm this,

> "Emblems are we of joy or woe,
> And tender recollections glow,
> Inspired by our name."

PERUVIAN HELIOTROPE (*Heliotropium peruvianum*). —INFATUATION. I LOVE YOU.

> "Qui voit ta fleur en boira le poison !
> Elle a donné des sens à la sagesse,
> Et des désirs à la froide raison."—BERNIS.

THE natives of the East say that perfumes lift them up to heaven. It is certain that they stimulate us, and produce most pleasurable sensations. The impression they make upon us is so strong, that, if once associated with any remarkable event in life, whether joyful or sorrowful, the same perfume will, after a long series of years, revive all the sensations we at that time experienced. Several instances of this have been recorded, and probably no reader of these lines will be found who has not felt the truth of it.

The illustrious botanist Jussieu, while herbarizing in the Cordilleras, became suddenly sensible of a most delicious fragrance. He began to expect that he should find some brilliant flowers, but he saw only some pretty herbaceous plants, of a pleasant green, from which hung loosely spikes of a pale blue colour. He drew near the shrubs, and observed that the flowers with which they were laden turned towards the sun, which they seemed to him as regarding with devotion. Struck with this disposition of the flowers, he gave the plant the name of Heliotrope (the name he formed of the two Greek words, $\tau\rho o\pi\acute{e}\omega$, *I turn*, and $\mathring{\eta}\lambda\iota o\varsigma$, *the sun*) ; the flower turning itself to the sun.

The learned botanist, delighted with his newly found plant, applied himself to collect some of its seeds, and sent them to the Jardin du Roi, where they germinated, and the plants thrived and put forth their bloom. The ladies welcomed this flower with rapture ; they placed it in their choicest vases, they called it the plant of love, and received with cold indifference every proffered bouquet which did not contain this favourite flower. It was under the high auspices of the fairest and loveliest of Nature's works, that the Peruvian Heliotrope, grown for the first time at Paris, in 1740, made a successful *début* on that continent, and has since spread itself throughout the whole of Europe.

A very amiable lady, who was passionately fond of the

Heliotrope, being one day asked what charm a flower so melancholy and so devoid of splendour could possess in her eyes, replied, "The perfume of the Heliotrope is to my parterre what mind is to beauty, what joy is to love, and what love is to youth."

An anonymous writer has thus sung of its habit of turning to the sun,

> "There is a flower whose modest eye
> Is turned with looks of light and love,
> Who breathes her softest, sweetest sigh,
> Whene'er the sun is bright above."

PHEASANT'S-EYE (*Adonis autumnalis*).—SORROWFUL REMEMBRANCES.

THIS, one of the very few scarlet flowers indigenous in England, has found its way into the border, where it reminds us continually of the fate of Adonis, saying, as it were,

> "Look, in the garden blooms the Flos Adonis,
> And memory keeps of him who rashly died,
> Thereafter changed by Venus, weeping, to this flower."

La Fontaine named one of his poems after this unfortunate youth, in which he writes,

> "Je n'ai jamais chanté que l'ombrage des bois,
> Flore, Echo, les zéphirs et leurs molles haleines,
> Le vert tapis des prés et l'argent des fontaines.
> C'est parmi les forêts qu'a vécu mon héros ;
> C'est dans les bois qu'Amour a troublé son repos.

Ma muse en sa faveur de myrte s'est parée :
J'ai voulu célébrer l'amant de Cythérée,
Adonis, dont la vie eut des termes si courts,
Qui fut pleuré des Ris, qui fut plaint des Amours."

All the readers of ancient mythology know that the beautiful youth Adonis was killed by a wild boar. It was for his sake that Venus left the pleasures of Cythera ; and she shed bitter tears on account of his sad fate. Her tears were not in vain. The earth received them with the blood of Adonis, and forthwith brought forth a small plant that decked itself with flowers which resembled drops of blood. Venus found Adonis dead, and while she was wailing and weeping, Shakspeare says,

" By this, the boy that by her side lay killed
Was melted like a vapour from her sight,
And in his blood, that on the ground lay spilled,
A purple flower sprung up, chequered with white,
    Resembling well his pale cheeks, and the blood
    Which in round drops upon their whiteness stood."

Lustrous and transient flowers, too faithful emblems of life, you were dedicated by Beauty herself to Sorrowful Remembrances!

THE PIMPERNEL (*Anagallis arvensis*).—Assignation.

THE name Anagallis is said by some to be derived from ἀνάγειν, *to draw back*, because the most common kind was found useful in drawing arrow-heads from wounds ; by others

from ἀναγέλαειν, *to laugh again,* because its medicinal virtues
. cleansed the liver, and so removed causes of despondency and
low spirits, as to restore cheerfulness. The flower is associated with cheerfulness, for when it is fully expanded the
weather is always bright, the air is dry and reviving, and that
at a season when we have much of moisture in our atmosphere. It is one of those flowers which open and close at
stated times. In our latitude this expands punctually about
7.8 A.M., and closes at 2.3 P.M. It is also an hygrometer, for
when the air is very damp, its flowers do not open, or speedily
close again ; hence it is called the Shepherd's Weather-glass,
and according to its warning voice he may make his appoint-
ments. The author of Favourite Field Flowers, speaking as
a Shepherd might be supposed to do, says,

" And if I would the weather know, ere on some pleasure trip I go,
My Scarlet Weather-Glass will show, whether it will be fair or no.
The blue-eyed Pimpernel will tell, by closed lids of rain and showers ;
A fine bright day is known full well, when open wide it spreads its
    flowers.
Some flowers put on more gay attire, and this in usefulness excel.
But I, a Shepherd, most admire the blue-eyed Scarlet Pimpernel."

THE PINE TREE.—DARING.

THIS tree seems to disdain our quiet groves, and to prefer
bathing its head in the moisture of the clouds above, and to
feel its foliage continually buffeted by the winds, when its
branches give utterance to sounds like the murmurs of the

ocean, or like that caused by the surging billows as they toss about among the rocks,

"The loud wind through the forest wakes
With sounds like ocean roaring, wild and deep,
And in yon gloomy Pines strange music makes,
Like symphonies unearthly, heard in sleep ;
The sobbing waters wash their waves and weep,
Where moans the blast its dreary path along,
The bending Firs a mournful cadence keep."—DRUMMOND.

Thus daring is the Pine, attaining some eighty feet in height, and taking for its starting-point the loftiest elevations where vegetation may be found. Again, when the "lords of the creation" wish to plough the main, they cut down Chaucer's "sailing Firre," and Spenser's "sayling Pine," and Browne's

"Pine, with whom men through the ocean venture,"

to effect their design. Hart, translating Statius, calls the Pine itself,

"The adventurous Fir, that sails the vast profound."

So daring is this tree that it braves both the winds of heaven, and the raging waters of the deep abyss of ocean.

THE PINE APPLE (*Bromelia Ananas*).—YOU ARE PERFECT.

THE Pine Apple has not been known to us much more than a century and a half. It is decidedly the first fruit in the world. Surrounded by handsome leaves, it resembles an

158

apple (fir-cone) of the Pine tree, sculptured in a solid mass of pale gold. It is so beautiful that it might seem to be made to delight the eye, so delicious that one may fancy it unites in itself the sweetness and richness of all other fruits, and so fragrant, that we might be induced to cultivate it for its perfume only.

THE PINK *(Dianthus prolifer).*—Lively and Pure Affection.

"The Pink can no one justly slight, the gardener's favourite flower;
He sets it now beneath the light, now shields it from its power."—
Goethe.

THE Wild Pink is single, red, and odoriferous. Cultivation has added to the number of its petals, and variations in colour. These beautiful flowers paint themselves in an infinity of shades, from light rose to pure white, from deep red to the hue of glowing fire. The same flower puts on contrasting, yet blending tints. Pure white is pricked with crimson, and the rose-colour is streaked with a vivid and brilliant red. Then they are marbled, spotted, and again sharply cut, so that the eye is led to fancy that in the calyx there is an alabaster and a purple flower. Again, the Pink is nearly as varied in form as in colour. It opens its pretty flower-work as a tuft, a cockade, a boss, and at other times it assumes the shape of the rose. It always retains its delicious odour, and it constantly strives to divest itself of its artificial dress, and to resume its simple attire. For the hand of the gardener, which can double and triple its petals, variegate and diversify its colour, does not know how to render his changes constant. Thus Nature has sown in our heart the delightful germ of feeling. Art and Society, in developing and cultivating this germ, improve, weaken, or elevate it. A hundred causes combining together can make these effects inconstant and changeable ; but, notwithstanding the caprices, the errors, and the incomprehensible workings of the human heart, Nature ultimately brings back the feelings and opinions into their proper channel. Rochefoucauld has said, "It is with true love as with a spectral appearance : all the world speaks of it, but few or none have seen it !" What does this fretful moralist understand by true love ? Does he wish to make us believe that true love is a chimera ? No, true love lives in our hearts ; but

> " J'ai vu l'amour pourtrait en divers lieux :
> L'un le peint vieil, cruel et furieux ;
> L'autre plus doux, enfant, aveugle, nu ;
> Chacun le tient pour tel qu'il l'a connu
> Par ses bienfaits ou par sa forfaiture.
> Pour mieux au vrai défini sa nature,
> C'est que chacun varie en son cerveau
> Un dieu d'amour pour lui propre et nouveau.
> Et qu'il y a dans les entendemens
> D'amours autant que de sortes d'amans."—HERCET.

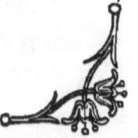

THE PLANE TREE (*Platanus orientalis*).—GENIUS.

THERE was a long avenue of superb Plane Trees at Athens, whither the Greeks used to resort. They also paid a species of reverence or religious worship to these magnificent trees, which they dedicated to good genii and the pleasures of the mind.

THE PLUM TREE (*Prunus domestica*).—KEEP YOUR PROMISES.

EVERY year our Plum Trees cover themselves with an abundance of flowers, but if the luxuriant growth of the trees is not pruned by the able hand of a skilful fruit-grower, they will not give us, the fruit they promise, more than once in three years.

POET'S NARCISSUS (*Narcissus poetica*).—EGOTISM.

THE Poet's Narcissus emits a pleasing perfume ; it carries a golden crown in the middle of a large flower of ivory whiteness, gently bending down. This plant seems natural to our climate ; it delights in shade and in the freshness of the river's rim.

The ancients saw in this flower the metamorphosis of a young shepherd, whom Love punished for his indifference by a fatal mistake. A thousand nymphs fancied the handsome Narcissus, and they learnt to know the pains of unrequited love. Echo was treated with coldness by the ungrateful youth. She was then beautiful; but grief and reproach effaced her beauty; her substance wasted until she resembled a skeleton; the gods pitied her, and changed her bones into stones, but they could not heal her mind, which still bewailed her lot in the remote places whither she followed so often the cruel-hearted shepherd who could not return her love.

Wearied by the chace and the intense heat which scorched the earth, the handsome Narcissus lay down to rest on the thick grass, at the brink of a fountain whose waters had never been disturbed. The shepherd, attracted by its coolness, wished to quench his thirst; he bent over the pure crystal of the treacherous wave; there he saw himself, whom he at once admired, and, struck with his own image, and gazing intently upon the reflection, he lost the power of motion, and was like a statue fixed upon the bank. Love, who avenges himself on the rebellious heart, adorned the reflected image with all the attractions he can bestow; then he mocked the mad mistake, abandoning his victim to the delirium which consumed him. Echo alone saw his pain, his tears; she alone heard his sighs and the insensate vows addressed to himself. Still, full of tenderness, the nymph answered his complaints, and repeated his last adieus, which were not for her; even while expiring, the unhappy youth continued searching for, at the bottom of the water, the illusion which had enchanted him; and descending into the shades he sought it again in the dark waters of the Styx, from whose banks nothing could draw him away. The naiads, his sisters, bewailed his death, and covered his body with their long hair ; they besought the dryads to raise a wood pile for his funeral rites. Echo followed the nymphs and repeated their plaints with disconsolate voice. The funeral pile was raised, but the body, which it was to reduce to ashes, was gone; there was found in place of it, a pale and melancholy flower, which even now droops over fountains of water as Narcissus drooped over the Stygian wave.

From that day the Eumenides have adorned their terrible brows with flowers dedicated to Egotism, which is of all follies the saddest and most fatal.

The fable of Narcissus has been supposed, by Keats, to have originated in the fancy of a poet. He asks,

> " What first inspired a bard of old to sing
> Narcissus pining o'er the untainted spring ? "

And then he answers,

> " In some delicious ramble he had found
> A little space, with boughs all woven round ;
> And in the midst of all a clearer pool
> Than e'er reflected in its pleasant cool
> The blue sky, here and there, serenely peeping,
> Through tendril wreaths fantastically creeping.
> And on the bank a lonely flower he spied,
> A meek and forlorn flower, with nought of pride,
> Drooping its beauty o'er the watery clearness,
> To woo its own sad image into nearness :
> Deaf to light Zephyrus it would not move,
> But still would seem to droop, to pine, to love.

So while the poet stood in this sweet spot,
Some fainter gleamings o'er his fancy shot ;
Nor was it long ere he had told the tale
Of young Narcissus, and sad Echo's vale."

Shelley, admiring the flower, wrote,

" And Narcissi, the fairest among them all—
Who gaze on their eyes in the stream's recess,
Till they die of their own dear loveliness !"

THE POLIANTHES (*P. tuberosa*).—VOLUPTUOUSNESS.

THIS beautiful and most odoriferous flower, commonly known as the Tuberose, and which is calculated to please all, was brought from Persia in 1632. It flowered for the first time in France, at M. de Peiresc's, at Beaugencier, near Toulon. The flower was then single ; but its petals became double after some time, under the careful hand of Lecour, of Leyden. From that place it spread every where. In Russia it blooms only for royalty, and those who come near the court. It is naturalized in Peru ; there it grows without culture, and combines with the brilliant capucin to decorate the fair American. The Tuberose, that superb native of the East, which the illustrious Linnæus has named Polianthes, from the abundance of its flowers, a flower worthy of cities, has become with us, as it is in Persia, the emblem of Voluptuousness. A young Icoglan, who receives from the hands of his mistress a stem of the Tuberose in bloom, experiences supreme happiness ;

for he knows that he may thus interpret the happy symbol of their mutual affection;

" Our happiness will surpass our anxieties."

All the world knows and admires the white spikes and stars of the Tuberose ; those beautiful spikes are the termination of a tall and slender stem, and they diffuse a most penetrating and intoxicating perfume. Shelley says of it,

" the sweet tuberose,
The sweetest flower for scent, that blows ; "

and Moore tells us how it is esteemed by the Malays, who call it Sandal Malam, or the Mistress of the Night ;

" The Tuberose, with her silvery light,
That in the gardens of Malay
Is called the Mistress of the Night."

THE POMEGRANATE (*Punica granatum*).—
FOPPISHNESS.

FOPPISHNESS has been represented by the figure of an ignorant person, who would force one to admire the brilliancy of a bouquet of Pomegranate flowers, which, fine in their appearance though inodorous, have sometimes been used as the emblem of Folly.

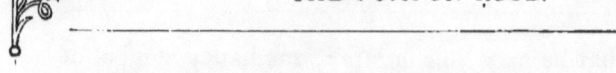

THE POMPON ROSE (*R. M. Pomponia*).—LOVELINESS.

LOVELINESS or Gracefulness, which is the great charm of early childhood, forms the principal attraction of the Pompon Rose.

THE POTATO (*Solanum tuberosum*).—BENEVOLENCE.

THE Potato is alike esteemed by the rich and the poor. It is a luxury to the former, and constitutes a large part of the food of the latter. It is a food which escapes the greediness of the monopolist, who, because the tubers will not keep well, so as to be *good* for food, longer than from the ripening of one crop to the planting of another, cannot withhold it as he may do corn. Like true charity, it is an unassuming plant, hiding its treasures in the earth, and preparing itself for our use, with very little effort on our part to cultivate it. America has supplied us with this root, which for ever has banished from Europe that most frightful of plagues, famine. How important it is to the inhabitants of the United Kingdom, those know who remember the failure of the crops in Ireland in 1846 or 1847. Sir Walter Raleigh is believed to have been the means of its importation into England.

THE PRIMROSE (*Primula vulgaris*).—EARLY YOUTH.

BURNS says, " The Primrose I will pu', the firstling of the year," which, in truth, it is, when we speak of the wild flowers of our native country ; and it proclaims to us that

166

period in which Winter, withdrawing herself, sees the hem of her snowy mantle adorned with an embroidery of verdure and of flowers. It is no longer the season for frosts, nor yet are bright days come. Yet how exhilarating are the days when Primrose tufts appear on every bank, and beneath every hedgerow! How well do we remember the millions which deck the hill-sides, and vales, and hazel copses in the lovely country about Godalming! there, mingled with the dog-violet and a vast variety of wild flowers, they are a most fitting emblem of Early Youth, when the spirits are full of freshness, when hope abounds, when the future is all of a rosy tint, when the mind is free from anything like real care or sorrow in most of us! And in that beautiful spot these lovely flowers have an added charm in the presence of the nightingale, whose rich and liquid notes fill the air in every direction at the joyous season of Spring; well may Bidlake say to the Primrose,—

" Pale visitant of balmy Spring, joy of the new-born year,
That bidd'st young hope new plume his wing, soon as thy buds appear.
  * * * * * *
Remote from towns thy transient life is spent in skies more pure ;
The suburb smoke, the seat of strife, thou can'st but ill endure.
  * * * * * *
Thy smiles young innocence invite, what time thy lids awake,
In shadowy lane to taste delight, or mazy tangled brake.
  * * * * * *
Ah ! happy breasts ! unknown to pain, I would not spoil your joys,
Nor vainly teach you to complain of life's delusive toys.
Be jocund still, still sport and smile, nor dream of woe or future guile ;
    For soon shall ye awakened find
The joys of life's sad thorny way, but fading flowerets of a day
    Cut down by every wind." ,

PRIVET (*Ligustrum vulgare*).—PROHIBITION.

THE hawthorn hedge is a real protection, when well kept, against horses, cattle, and sheep, and against man generally. The Privet is prohibitory, and is a sufficient guard against injury, to that which it surrounds, from the well-meaning, and those who act on the golden rule of doing unto others what they would that others should do to them. It forms a pretty fence, being evergreen for nine months of the year, bearing a pretty white flower in season, and a small black berry ; but it requires care, for there is nothing which sooner becomes denuded of its foliage by the absence of air and light.

THE PUMPKIN (*Cucurbita Pepo*).—BULKINESS.

THE Pumpkin is usually very large, and of considerable weight. It is sometimes said of a very stout person, that he resembles a Pumpkin. The comparison is vulgar, and cannot fail to be taken as an affront.

THE PYRAMIDAL BELL FLOWER (*Campanula pyramidalis*).—CONSTANCY.

THE stems of this very ornamental plant sometimes exceed six feet in height. These stems are studded from bottom to top with large and beautiful flowers, which begin to bloom in July, and continue to display their beauty until October. The splendid colour of these pyramidal clusters is a lovely blue, the colour of the eye of a young lady whose characteristic is constancy.

RED AND WHITE ROSES.—WARMTH OF HEART.

THE poet Bonnefons sent to the object of his affection two Roses, one deep red, the other white. The Red Rose was the symbol of his heart, which was being consumed by the intensity of his anxiety, the other told of the pallor of his countenance, caused by the exhausting force of his internal fire. He sent with the Roses the following lines :

> " Pour toi, Daphné, ces fleurs viennent d'éclore ;
> Vois, l'une est blanche, et l'autre se colore
> D'un vif éclat : l'une peint ma pâleur,
> L'autre mes feux ; toutes deux mon malheur."

Carew, who lived 1580-1639, has thus interpreted the language of the Red and White Rose together,—

> " Read in these Roses the sad story,
> Of my hard fate, and your own glory ;
> In the white you may discover
> The paleness of a fainting lover ;
> In the red the flames still feeding
> On my heart with fresh wounds bleeding.
> The white will tell you how I languish,
> And the red express my anguish,
> The white my innocence displaying,
> The red my martyrdom betraying :
> The frowns that on your brow resided,
> Have those roses thus divided.
> Oh ! let your smiles but clear the weather,
> And then they both shall grow together."

In our own national history, the union of the Red Rose and the White, is the emblem of a return to that state of feeling which ought to exist among all mankind, and especially among those of the same race and nation. Long had the two Roses represented the rival houses of York and Lancaster, each anxious to do battle to the death, each burning with hatred to the other, until a better mind came, when the two combined worked together for the good of the Commonwealth. Wordsworth sings of this happy change,

> " The Red Rose is a gladsome flower.
> Her thirty years of winter past, the Red Rose is revived at last ;
> She lifts her head for endless Spring, for everlasting blossoming ;
> Both Roses flourish, Red and White ; in love and sisterly delight,
> The two that were at strife are blended, and all old troubles now are
> ended."

RED VALERIAN (*Valeriana montana*).—READINESS.

THIS species of Valerian has been brought from Switzerland within a hundred years. Its attire is bright, but always lax. This mountain child retains, amid our cultivated flowers, her rustic bearing, which imparts the air of a *parvenu*. This wild beauty owes her good fortune to merit; the root is a remedy for those maladies which engender feebleness; an infusion of the plant strengthens the sight, revivifies the spirits, and drives away melancholy. The flowers continue to bloom for a long time. Cultivation improves the flower, but the plant does not despise its origin, for it abandons our borders to dwell on the side of a dry hill, or on the top of

a ruined wall. The indigenous Valerians of our fields and woods possess as many virtues and beauties as this; but the gardener neglects them, because they do not offer the same readiness and facility to his nurturing hand.

REEDS.—Music.

"the mingling sounds that come,
Of shepherd's ancient reed."—Moore.

PAN, who was devotedly fond of the fair Syrinx, pursued her one day upon the banks of the river Ladon, in Arcadia. The nymph intreated the river to help her, when she was received into the stream, and became transformed into Reeds. Pan cut several of the Reeds, of different sizes, and formed of them, as we are told, the first shepherd's pipe. Moore tells us that this is still a pastoral instrument of music in Syria.

REST HARROW (*Ononis spinosa*).—Obstacle.

THIS pretty weed may still be found in some parts of the country, although the intelligent and industrious farmer has used his best efforts to banish it. It has strong woody roots, which, when it abounded, were a great obstacle to the steady progress of the plough, as its thorny branches were to the motion of the harrow. As food it may be said to be generally rejected by all animals except the ass, whence its generic name.

THE ROCK ROSE.—SAFETY.

THE Cistus, or Rock Rose, bears some resemblance to Chick Pea. Aristotle tells us that it is a powerful protection against ghosts and phantoms, when held in the hand. The petals of the flowers of *C. villosus*, are purple, large, and spread open like the Rose. They commonly fall off on the same day on which they open, a feature which Campbell notes :

> " Thou wert working late, thou busy busy bee !
> After the fall of the Cistus flower."

There is, however, a succession of new flowers daily for a considerable time in May and June. In September and October, also, they will bloom again, if the autumn be mild ; and their flowers may be procured in winter by sheltering the plants from frost.

THE ROSE.—BEAUTY.

WHO, that has ever been endowed with the power of song, has not sung of the Rose? Poets have not been able to exaggerate her beauty, nor to sing her praises to perfection. They have spoken of her, and with justice, as the daughter of the sky, the ornament of the earth, and the glory of Spring ; but what words have ever expressed the charms of this lovely flower, her exquisite beauty, her matchless grace ? When she spreads open her petals, the eye follows her harmonious outlines with delight. But how can we describe the rounded sections which form her entirety, the lovely tints so delicately laid upon her, the sweet perfume which she sends forth ? Behold her, in the Spring, raising herself softly amid her elegant foliage, surrounded by her many buds ; one might say that the Queen of flowers sports with the air which plays around her, that she adorns herself with diamond-like drops of dew which bathe her, that she smiles at the sun's rays which persuade her to display her charms. Nature seems to have exhausted her resources, in order to lavish upon her to excess, freshness, beauty of form, perfume, splendour, and loveliness. The Rose decorates the whole earth ; she is one of the most common of flowers.

On the day that the beauty of the Rose is perfected, it begins to fade ; but each succeeding Spring restores her to us fresh and new. Poets have sung of her charms in vain ; they have not made her praises grow old or become wearisome ; and her name of itself keeps their productions fresh and attractive. The emblem of every age ; the interpreter of all our sentiments; the Rose is mixed up with our festivals, with our joys and our sorrows. Innocent mirth crowns herself with Roses ; simple modesty borrows her blushing tints ; and we bestow a wreath of Roses as the reward of virtue. The Rose is the image of youth, innocence, and harmless pleasure. She belongs to Venus, and even is the rival of her beauty ; the Rose possesses, like her, charms more lovely than beauty. Moore has sung rapturously of the Rose,

" Rose! thou art the sweetest flower, that ever drank the amber shower ;
Rose! thou art the fondest child of dimpled Spring, the wood-nymph
    wild ! "

and again,

" While we invoke the wreathed Spring, resplendent Rose ! to thee we'll
    sing ;
Resplendent Rose, the flower of flowers, whose breath perfumes Olym-
    pus' bowers ;
Whose virgin blush, of chasten'd dye, enchants so much our mortal
    eye."

and further,

" The Rose distils a healing balm, the beating pulse of pain to calm ;
Preserves the cold inurnèd clay, and mocks the vestige of decay;
And when at length in pale decline, its florid beauties fade and pine,
Sweet as in youth, its balmy breath diffuses odour e'en in death !"

We are told that all Roses were once white, and Herrick
accounts for some being changed into red, thus,

"'Tis said, as Cupid danced among the gods, he down the nectar flung ;
Which on the white rose being shed, made it for ever after red."

Moore, however, makes the origin of the red Rose coeval
with the rising of Venus (Aphrodite) from the foam of the
sea ; he says,

" Then, then, in strange eventful hour, the earth produced an infant
    flower,
Which sprung, with blushing tinctures drest, and wantoned o'er its
    parent breast.
The gods beheld this brilliant birth, and hailed the Rose, the boon of
    earth !
With nectar drops, a ruby tide, the sweetly orient buds they dyed,
And bad them on the spangled.thorn expand their bosoms to the morn."

The same writer in his Irish Melodies, gives another statement:

"They tell us that-Love in his fairy bower,
Had two blush Roses, of birth divine ;
He sprinkled the one with a rainbow's shower,
But bathed the other with mantling wine.

Soon did the buds, that drank of the floods
Distilled by the rainbow, decline and fade ;
While those which the tide of ruby had dyed
All blushed into beauty, like thee, sweet maid!"

THE ROSE ACACIA (*Robinia hispida*).—ELEGANCE.

A HANDSOME shrub when grown in a sheltered situation.
The toilet has nothing of greater freshness, nor of greater
elegance, than the attire of this pretty shrub. Its inclining
attitude, its gay green, its beautiful rose-coloured branches,
which have the appearance of waving ribands, all give it the
appearance of a coquette arrayed in ball-room dress.

THE HUNDRED-LEAVED ROSE.—THE GRACES.

WHEN the three Graces are spoken of as being in attendance
on Venus and her Cupids, they are said to be crowned with
Myrtle ; when they accompany the Muses, they are represented as wearing wreaths of Roses.

A ROSE IN A TUFT OF GRASS.—THERE IS EVERY THING TO BE GAINED BY GOOD COMPANY.

"ONE day," said the poet Sadi, "I saw a rose-bush surrounded by a tuft of grass. 'What!' I cried, 'does that vile plant dare to place itself in the company of Roses?' I was about to tear the grass away, when it meekly addressed me, saying, 'Spare me! I am not the Rose, it is true; but, from my perfume, any one may know at least that I have lived with Roses.'" How anxiously should we seek the company of those whose intellectual and moral character surpasses our own, that we may drink in some of their mind's wealth and moral worth, and so far be improved by the association.

A ROSE-BUD.—YOUNG GIRL.

A YOUNG girl is to beautiful womanhood, what the Rose-bud is to the Rose in the perfection of its charms. Burns made use of the Rose-bud as the emblem of a favourite young lady in a poetical address to "dear little Jessie," whose father was a master in the Edinburgh High school, he says,

> " Beauteous rose-bud, young and gay, blooming in thy early May,
> Never may'st thou, lovely flower, chilly shrink in sleety shower.
> May'st thou long, sweet crimson gem, richly deck thy native stem;"

and again, to the same,

" Thus thou, sweet Rose-bud, young and gay,
   Shall beauteous blaze upon the day,
   And bless the parent's evening ray,
      That watched thy early morning."

A ROSE LEAF.—I AM NEVER IMPORTUNATE.

AT Amadan, there was a school of philosophers, whose statutes prescribed that, "the Academicians should think much, write little, and speak as little as possible." Dr. Zeb, famous throughout the East, learnt that there was a vacancy in the academy, and hastened to seek it, but, unfortunately, arrived too late. The members were extremely sorry. They had just accorded to influence that which was due to merit. The president, not knowing how to express a refusal which caused the assembly to blush with shame, had a cup brought to him, which he filled so full of water that one drop more would have made it run over the brim. The learned candidate understood by this that they had not now room for him. He was withdrawing, sadly disappointed, when he saw a Rose Leaf at his feet. On this his courage revived. He took up the leaf and placed it so lightly upon the surface of the water in the cup, that not a single drop was displaced. At this display of his ingenuity, the whole assembly clapped their hands, and the doctor was received, by acclamation, among the number of the silent Academicians.

ROSEMARY (*Rosmarinus officinalis*).—Your Presence Revives me.

HUNGARY water is said to be distilled from Rosemary, which is refreshing in its fragrance. It was formerly thought to give vigour to the nervous system, to remove headache, and to strengthen the memory, on which account Shakspeare wrote,—

"There's Rosemary—that's for remembrance; 'pray you, love, remember;'"

Rosemary was also deemed the emblem of Fidelity between lovers, and so was worn at weddings. It symbolized repentance, and hence its adoption at funerals, as in Wales and Cheshire. At such times a few stalks are bound together and presented to each of the mourners, who, when the departed friend is consigned to the grave, cast in their bunches upon the coffin, thereby expressing, as we presume, their faithful and lasting remembrance of the dead. Kirke White addresses it as a funeral flower,

" Come, funeral flower ! who lov'st to dwell
With the pale corpse in lonely tomb,
*   *   *   *   *
My grave shall be in yon lone spot,
Where, as 1 lie, by all forgot,
A dying fragrance thou wilt o'er my ashes shed."

ROSE-SCENTED GERANIUM (*Pelargonium capitatum*).—PREFERENCE.

THERE are numberless species of the Geranium, or Pelargonium. Some are heavy, others bright ; some perfumed, others scentless. The Rose-scented kind is distinguished by the smoothness of its leaves, its agreeable fragrance, and its pretty purplish flowers.

RUSHES (*Juncus conglomeratus*).—DOCILITY.

"YIELDING and tractable as a Rush," is an old proverb. Very useful are different species of this genus, and they are so pliant that we may work them into any form we please.

SAFFRON (*Crocus sativus*).—DO NOT DECEIVE YOURSELVES.

A LIGHT infusion of Saffron tends to raise the spirits ; but if indulged in to excess it produces intoxication. If its emanations be inhaled in moderation, it is said to be restorative ; if too freely breathed, the effect is injurious.

SAGE (*Salvia officinalis*).—ESTEEM.

VARIOUS species of this genus are of much value. At one time our garden Sage was of high repute as a medicine, as a sudorific, aromatic, astringent, and antiseptic. For these and other supposed properties, it is not improperly the emblem of that Esteem which it has acquired.

THE SCARLET GERANIUM.—FOLLY.

MADAME DE STAEL was always angry when any one tried to introduce into her society a mindless man. One day, however, a friend of hers risked the introduction of a young Swiss officer of very pleasing figure. The lady, misled by his appearance, became animated, and uttered a thousand pleasant remarks to the new comer, who at first seemed dumb with surprise and admiration. But, since he listened in silence for an hour, she began to doubt the cause of his conduct, and all at once addressed him with such direct questions, that it was quite necessary that he should answer. Alas! the unfortunate fellow could reply with nothing but foolish nonsense. M. de Staël then turned away, vexed at her loss of pains and mental effort, and, addressing herself to her friend, said, "Truly, sir, you are like my gardener, who thought to give me a treat by bringing me this morning a pot of Geraniums; but I tell you that I sent the flower away, desiring him never to let me see it again." "Ah! why so?" asked the young man in astonishment. "It is, sir, since you wish to know it, because the Geranium is a flower well clad in scarlet: so long as we look at it, it pleases the eye; but when we press it lightly, it emits a disagreeable odour." While saying this, the lady rose and went out, leaving, as we may well imagine,

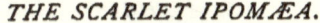
the cheeks of the young officer as red as his regimentals, which were the colour of the flower to which he had been compared.

The scarlet Geranium is a most pleasing object in beds on our lawns, displaying its masses of brilliant flowers to great advantage in the later Summer months.

THE SCARLET IPOMŒA (*I. coccinea*).—I ATTACH
MYSELF TO YOU.

LIKE other weak twining plants, the Scarlet Ipomœa has need of a support to hold up its slender branches, which, without being burdensome to its supporters, surrounds them with verdure and flowers.

SCRATCH WEED, OR BED STRAW (*Galium verum*).—
HARDNESS.

BED Straw was sometimes used to strew upon beds because of its agreeable fragrance. Scratch Weed seems to be another species, once thought to be of great utility, but now sought to be banished from fields, an attempt which its tenacity of life, or hardness, renders most difficult. The effort to eradicate it is continuous, but the plant as persistently maintains its position.

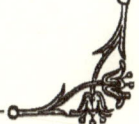

SEA THRIFT (*Statice maritima*).—SYMPATHY.

" From the border lines,
Composed of daisy and resplendent Thrift,
Flowers straggling forth had on those paths encroached,
Which they were used to deck."—WORDSWORTH.

The generic name of this plant is Greek, and denotes
that which has the property of fixing, uniting, and retain-
ing. The flowers are small, very numerous, turning towards
the sky, forming pretty purple blue spikes. They are very
ornamental border flowers, but require considerable care.
Naturally the plants prefer marshy places, and especially
the shores of the sea, where they seem to bind the sands
together by their abundant roots.

THE SENSITIVE PLANT (*Mimosa sensitiva*).— BASHFULNESS.

THE sensitive plant seems to shrink from under the hand
when about to touch it. At the slightest shock the leaflets
bend one towards another in succession. Then the common
leaf stalk, if the plant be low, bends down to the earth. A
cloud passing between it and the sun suffices to change the
position of the leaves and the whole appearance of the plant.
The ancients observed the phenomenon. Pliny speaks of it,
but neither Pliny, nor yet modern botanists have been able
satisfactorily to explain it. A Dr. Dutrochet made a variety

of experiments, the results of which satisfied himself, but do not appear to have convinced others. Shelley has written some lively verses about the plant, from which we extract a few lines :—

" A Sensitive Plant in a garden grew,
And the young winds fed it with silver dew,
And it opened its fan-like leaves to the light,
And closed them beneath the kisses of Night.
       *   *   *   *   *   *
—the Sensitive Plant, which could give small fruit
Of the love which it felt from the leaf to the root,
Received more than all [flowers], it loved more than ever,
Where none wanted but it, could belong to the giver—

For the Sensitive Plant has no bright flower ;
Radiance and odour are not its dower ;
It loves, even like Love, its deep heart is full,
It desires what it has not, the beautiful !
       *   *   *   *   *   *
Each and all like ministering angels were
For the Sensitive Plant sweet joy to bear,
Whilst the lagging hours of the day went by
Like windless clouds o'er a tender sky.

And when evening descended from heaven above,
And the earth was all rest, and the air was all love,
And delight, though less bright, was far more deep,
And the day's veil fell from the world of sleep,
       *   *   *   *   *   *
The Sensitive Plant was the earliest
Up-gathered into the bosom of rest ;
A sweet child weary of its delight;
The feeblest, and yet the favourite,
Cradled within the embrace of night."

THE SERPENTINE CACTUS (*C. Serpentinus*).— HORROR.

THIS species of Cactus throws its thorny stems, which bear a strong resemblance to serpents, in every direction. Its un-expected appearance within view, produces a slight sense of that Horror which we should feel, if a living reptile of a deadly nature were suddenly before us.

THE SERVICE TREE (*Pyrus domestica*).—PRUDENCE.

EVERY tree and every plant has its own peculiar phy-siognomy which seems to give it character. The thoughtless almond tree hastens to display her flowers in the Spring, at the risk of not bearing any fruit in the autumn, whilst the Service Tree, which comes forth more tardily, bears its fruit only when it has acquired its full strength; but then its crop is made sure. Hence it is the meet emblem of Prudence. This tree, so beautiful and so hardy, retains its shining red berries the winter through; we see them glittering in the midst of snows; it is a harvest which is yielded only in winter, and which Providence has kept in reserve for the smaller birds.

SHAKING SAINTFOIN (*Hedysarum Gyrans*).— AGITATION.

THIS wonderful plant is a native of Bengal, near the Ganges. No sooner do the ternate leaves of a seedling develop themselves, than they commence moving, now here, now there. In their native clime this motion does not cease so long as vitality exists. They do not observe any time, order, or direction in their movements. One leaflet will revolve, while all the others on the same footstalk are at rest. Now a few leaflets move about, then the others on that petiole. The whole plant is never agitated at the same time. The leaves are not quiescent even in winter. With us this agitation can only be detected about mid-day.

SMALL BINDWEED (*Convolvulus arvensis.*)—HUMILITY.

THIS pretty little Bindweed is one of the greatest favourites among our indigenous wild flowers. Its feeble stems cannot raise themselves above the surface of the earth, but trail upon it until some friendly plant lends its firm support. Then the lowly Bindweed twines around its friendly sustainer, and decorates it with its nicely-shaped green leaves and beautiful pale whitish-pink flowers. It is very common in our corn-fields, and is a certain indicator of a dry soil. It is a most fitting emblem of Humility.

SMALL CAPE MARIGOLD (*Calendula pluvialis*).— PRESAGE. OMEN.

THIS flower expands invariably at seven o'clock in the morning, and remains open until four o'clock in the afternoon, if the weather be dry. If the flower does not open, or if it closes before its appointed time, we may be sure that there will be rain during the day.

SMALL DOUBLE DAISY.—I RECIPROCATE YOUR AFFECTION.

IT would seem that the field daisy was long ago made double by cultivation, since in the days of chivalry it was a most expressive emblem. When the lady-love of a gallant knight granted him permission to emblazon his shield with a Double Daisy, it was a public avowal that she reciprocated his affection.

SNAP DRAGON (*Antirrhinum majus*).—PRESUMPTION.

THIS remarkable flower has singular attractions. Its colours are now very varied, and adorn our parterres. They need careful control in cultivation, for otherwise, like persons who are inclined to presume on the sufferance accorded them, they claim too large a space amid the company they are introduced to, and require either to be immediately banished, or for the future quietly passed over.

THE SNOWDROP (*Galanthus nivalis*).—CONSOLATION.

No sooner have we entered fully upon the Winter season, than the pale Snowdrop lifts up her white bells to assure us that Nature is not dead. The rude north wind may howl and sigh—the hoar frost may whiten the naked branches of our trees—the clouds may have covered the face of the earth with a snowy carpet—the songs of birds may have ceased, and the flowing streams may no longer murmur, being bound in icy fetters—the freezing atmosphere may have attained its maximum strength—the sun, shrouded in fog, may but feebly light up our fields—our hearts may sink saddened within us at the death-like appearance of Nature; but yet the springing up of the little Snowdrop produces an emotion of pleasure; the consolatory feeling that snow shall disappear, ice dissolve, birds renew their song, green leaves take the place of hoar frost, the sun shine forth again in splendour, and all Nature awaken to life and beauty.

The venerated Keble thus addressed the Snowdrop:

" Thou first-born of the year's delight, pride of the dewy glade,
In vernal green and virgin white, thy vestal robes arrayed.
      *   *   *   *   *   *   *
                     Thy shy averted smiles
To fancy bode a joyous year, one of life's fairy isles.

They twinkle to the wintry moon, and cheer the ungenial day,
And tell us, all will glisten soon as green and bright as they.

Is there a heart, that loves the Spring, their witness can refuse ? "

The answer is, No! and the poet goes on to moralize in a manner most devout and admirable, as those who love his " Christian Year " well know.

Langhorne addresses our flower as the

" Earliest bud that decks the garden, fairest of the fragrant race,
First-born child of vernal Flora, seeking mild thy lowly place ;

187

Though no warm or murmuring zephyr fan thy leaves with balmy wing,
Pleased we hail thee, spotless blossom, Herald of the infant Spring.

*   *   *   *   *   *   *   *

White, as falls the fleecy shower, thy soft form in sweetness grows ;
Not more fair the valley's treasure, not more sweet her lily blows.
Drooping harbinger of Flora, simply are thy blossoms drest ;
Artless as the gentle virtues mansioned in the blameless breast."

So pleasing is the appearance of the Snowdrop, when she
pierces through, and expands her flower over, the snow ; she
seems to cast a smile upon the severity of winter, and to say
to us, " I am come to calm your fears ; I am come to console
you in the absence of bright days, and to reassure you of
their return !"

SPIDER OPHRYS (*O. aranifera*).—Skill.

IDMON of Colophon was in great repute as a dyer. He
had a daughter Arachne, whose skill in weaving was such
that in her pride she challenged Minerva to a contest in the
art of weaving. Arachne wove a piece of cloth of so much
beauty that the goddess could not find any fault in it, but
tore it into pieces, at which the weaver was so grieved that she
hung herself. The rope was transformed into a cobweb, and
Arachne into a spider, from which we infer that man learnt
the weaving art from the spider, and first applied it in Lydia.
The flower is a remarkable production of Nature, being one
of those where she has produced in the vegetable kingdom,
an imitation of animal life. Here we see, as it were, upon a
plant the

" —skilful Spider seated silently,
  As lurking for his prey in webby bower ;"

Guillim, whose writings few know but all have read of in Scott's " Rob Roy," says "the Spider is free of the Weavers' Company."

SPIDERWORT (*Tradescantia virginica*).—TRANSIENT HAPPINESS.

A BLUE border-flower, but of no great beauty. The flower is said to continue in succession from April to October, fading on the day in which it opens.

THE SPINDLE TREE (*Euonymus europæa*).—YOUR CHARMS ARE TRACED UPON MY HEART.

THE wood of this tree was at one time used for spindles. Sculptors make use of it, as well as turners. It is also called prick-wood, from its being manufactured into skewers for a useful but not noble application. Hedges are formed of it sometimes, which in autumn are covered with rose-coloured berries producing a very pleasing effect.

SPOTTED ARUM (*A. maculatum*).—WARMTH.

THIS is known commonly as " Lords and Ladies," and is used both as food and medicine. If you taste the roots, they at first seem insipid, but afterwards the effect is as though

your tongue were pricked with needles, so acrid and sharp
is their juice. It is alleged by some naturalists, that the
spadix in certain of the species becomes so hot that the
hand cannot touch it with impunity. For one or the other
of these reasons it has been made the emblem of warmth.

SPURGE LAUREL (*Daphne Laureola*).—COQUETRY. DESIRE TO PLEASE.

THIS is valuable in shrubberies, thriving under the drip
of trees, and never attaining an unshapely size. Its bark is
such as to give it the appearance of a dead tree, but Nature,
to hide this deformity, envelopes its branches in purplish
flowers, and puts forth at the end a tuft of leaves resembling
a pine-apple in form.

The Spurge Laurel begins to flower amid the snows of
January ; it seems the fitting representative of an imprudent
coquette who, in the dead of winter, decks herself in Spring
attire.

SQUIRTING CUCUMBER (*Momordica Elaterium*).— CRITICISM.

ADVERSE criticism produces a painful effect upon the
unfortunate object of it, therefore the specific name of this
plant has suggested it as the proper symbol of the *biting*
operation.

THE STAR OF BETHLEHEM (*Ornithogalum umbellatum*).—PURITY.

THE " Bright-eyed Star of Bethlehem," is indigenous, but it is a welcome plant in our gardens. From April to June it bears an umbel of star-like flowers, white as the purest milk. There is no dweller in our borders more agreeable in its whole appearance than it, and none more pure and pleasing.

STRAWBERRY (*Fragaria vesca*).—PERFECT GOODNESS.

THE Strawberry Plant is a lowly one, but its leaves are exquisitely cut, and furnish, as regards form, ornaments on the coronets of the Princess Royal of England and her sisters, of Nephews of the royal blood, and of Dukes, Marquisses, and Earls. The flowers are pretty in shape, perfectly white, and cluster in masses upon the plants, and are so attractive as to induce children to pluck them; hence Wordsworth makes an elder child address a younger one thus :

" That is work of waste and ruin—do as Charles and I are doing !
　Strawberry blossoms, one and all, we must spare them—here are many;
　Look at it—the flower is small, small and low, though fair as any :
　Do not touch it ! summers two I am older, Anne, than you."

Then the child bids Anne pluck other flowers, whose fruit is useless to us, and proceeds to say why she would spare the Strawberry flower,

"God has given a kindlier power to the favoured Strawberry flower,
  When the months of Spring are fled, hither let us bend our walk ;
  Lurking berries ripe and red, there will hang on every stalk,
  Each within its leafy bower ; and for that promise spare that flower !"

And who would not join in the intreaty of the child to spare a flower which should produce so rich a fruit as the Strawberry, whose worth can only be expressed fully by the words, Perfect Excellence !

The good Bishop Mant, in his Wreath of April flowers, has not forgotten this, which he speaks of as,

"With milk-white flowers, whence soon shall swell
  Rich fruitage, to the taste and smell
  Pleasant alike, the Strawberry weaves
  Its coronets of three-fold leaves,
  In mazes through the sloping wood."

SUCCORY (*Cichorium Intybus*).—FRUGALITY.

THIS plant, and such like, were highly esteemed by the Egyptians, and we are told that they constitute half the food of that people of the present day. It was part of the repast of the poet Horace ; the leaves are much used by the French as a winter salad, and its roots enter largely into the compounds which are sold as coffee, in England ; to such an extent, indeed, that we have been assured by a most respectable dealer, that we never obtain *genuine* Coffee unless we specially stipulate for it when making a purchase. Succory, or Chicory as it is commonly called, is a cheap article, and hence its use is a frugal practice.

THE SUNFLOWER.—False riches.

This flower is from Peru, in which country it was formerly honoured as the image of the great orb of day.

It is related that a rich Lydian, named Pythias, owning gold mines, neglected to till his fields, that his slaves might work in the mines. His wife, who was wise and good, caused a dinner to be served with dishes of meats in gold, saying, " I give you the only thing in which you abound: you can reap only what you sow; think whether gold is so great a good !" He then saw that the annual productions of the earth were the true riches, distributed among men in return for their labour.

Longfellow has a poetical lesson of somewhat the same import. He says,

" As in at the gate we rode, behold,
A tower that was called the Tower of Gold !
For there the Kalif had hidden his wealth,
Heaped and hoarded and piled on high,
Like sacks of wheat in a granary;
And thither the miser crept by stealth
To feel of the gold that gave him health,
And to gaze and to gloat with his hungry eye
On the jewels that gleamed like a glow-worm's spark,
Or the eyes of a panther in the dark.

I said to the Kalif; ' Thou art old,
Thou hast no need of so much gold.
Thou should'st not have heaped and hidden it here,
Till the breath of battle was hot and near,
But have sown through the land these useless hoards,
To spring into shining blades of swords,

And keep thine honour swéet and clear.
These grains of gold are not grains of wheat,
These bars of silver thou canst not eat."

Gold, silver, and precious stones are but mediums of exchange ; hoarded up they are hurtful to the owner; spread, so as to help the struggling, to relieve the poor, to promote the glory of the Giver, they then become true riches, to be returned with interest into the bosom of the agent in their distribution.

SWEET BAY (*Laurus nobilis*).—TREACHERY.

IT was formerly a common practice in making custards, to throw into the pan a few leaves of Laurel, in order to flavour them. Where the party preparing them was well acquainted with the properties of the leaves, care was taken to limit the quantity so as to produce an agreeable flavour; but if too many were used they always produced a deleterious effect, and not seldom death has ensued where the quantity has been in excess ; hence the tree has been made emblematic of Treachery.

SWEET-SCENTED COLTSFOOT (*Tussilago fragrans*).
WE WILL DO YOU JUSTICE.

IT has always been the lot of men whose minds have soared above that of their contemporaries, to be unappreciated. Authors, poets, painters, inventors of surpassing merit, have rarely had the just value put upon their productions, and suggestions, and improvements in their life-time ; or, if otherwise, the recognition of their deserts has been too late to be of service to them. In these respects many plants have shared the lot of many men, and their value has long escaped the notice of those who were capable of appreciating them. Thus our plant, notwithstanding its agreeable fragrance, had for a long time grown at the foot of Mount Pila unknown. There it would have continued, doubtless, "to waste its sweets upon the desert air," if M. Villau, of Grenoble, had not discovered its good qualities. That botanist sang the praises of this humble flower ; he gave it a distinguished position in his writings ; and, from that time, it has been valued as an early blooming and fragrant flower, so that that degree of justice has been accorded to it which it deserves.

SWEET-SCENTED VIOLET (*Viola odorata*).—MODESTY.

LITTLE need be said to increase the universal admiration of this favourite flower, for there is not one more sought after than it, nor does any yield us greater pleasure when found in the early Spring. We admire the embossed leaves, the drooping purple flower, and are enchanted with its delicious fragrance. Then, as we roam through rustic lanes, or by the hedgerow, or the border of a wood, how pleasant it is to find that

> "Where the banks are wet with drops of morning dew,
> The gentle Violet steals out, in hood of blue ; "—TAYLOR.

or to see it when

> " Deep in the shade of a flowery vale,
> Its frail form waves in the passing gale ;"—ANON.

and then its rich purple, which Byron speaks of,

> " The sweetness of the Violet's deep blue eyes
> Kissed by the breath of heaven, seem coloured by the skies."

The fondness of this flower for the most retired spots, over-grown by grass, often in the very depth of the hawthorn hedge, where its presence can only be detected by the fragrance which Zephyr steals from her in passing, and diffuses through space, has made the Sweet-scented Violet the proper emblem of Modesty ; and so Miss Taylor sings of it,

> " Down in a green and shady bed, a modest Violet grew ;
> Its stalk was bent, it hung its head, as if to hide from view.
>
> And yet it was a lowly flower, its colour bright and fair ;
> It might have graced a rosy bower, instead of hiding there.
>
> Yet thus it was content to bloom, in modest tints arrayed ;
> And there diffused a sweet perfume, within the silent shade."

SWEET SULTAN (*Centaurea moschata*).—HAPPINESS.

IN the East, of which this handsome border flower is a native, the Sweet Sultan is considered the emblem of Supreme Happiness.

THE SYCAMORE (*Acer Pseudo-Platanus*).—RESERVE.

RESERVE is symbolized by the Sycamore Tree, which is slow to put forth its flowers. The tree is one of great beauty. We have had many self-sown, which, being allowed to remain in the spot where they were cradled, and with ample room to grow upward and laterally, have become natural specimens. They are very upright, well ramified, and altogether deserving of great admiration. They bloomed, and bore their seeds, furnished with two broad wings, in their seventeenth year.

THE TEASEL (*Dipsacus fullonum*).—MISANTHROPY.

IT is not easy to perceive why this should be the emblem of Misanthropy. It is a prickly plant, and requires two years from the time of being sown to grow to full ripeness. The prickly awns with which they are beset make the Teasel most useful, as being the best means known whereby clothiers are able to raise the nap upon our beautiful broadcloth.

TEN-WEEK STOCK (*Mathiola annua*).—PROMPTITUDE.

NO sooner have we cast the seeds of these pretty border flowers into the earth than they begin to germinate, and we quickly have them in masses, or borders covered with them. The bloom, however, is transient, so that we must sow for a succession from March to August. The pretty lilac, white, and rose-coloured tints of the flowers are fresh and various. This garden favourite diffuses an agreeable odour.

THE THISTLE (*Carduus nutans*).—STERNNESS.

THIS is, as is well known, the badge of the Scotch Order of the Thistle and St. Andrew, together with a gold chain interlaced with Thistle and rue. The motto of the Order is "Nemo me impune lacessit;" which, for our fair friends, we put into English, "No one annoys me with impunity;" a very suitable motto for Scotchmen in the days when the warlike spirit of their race was fully developed, by the invading attacks of relentless foes.

THORN APPLE (*Datura Stramonium*).—DECEITFUL CHARMS.

THE Thorn Apple has been compared to the capricious beauty who, unseen in the open light of day, sparkles only in the light which illuminates saloons and ball-rooms. There she displays her charms, and delighting in admiration, allures the young and ardent of the opposite sex, upon whom she has no heart to bestow. Some of the species have an agreeable odour, but they are poisonous; though others, in the hands of skilful practitioners, are useful.

THYME (*Thymus serpyllum*).—ACTIVITY.

THE Greeks regarded Thyme as the emblem of Activity. No doubt they observed that its perfume, which stimulates the brain, is very wholesome to elderly people, whose energies it seems to restore.

Action is characteristic of the soldier, and is always allied with true courage; wherefore, in days gone by, ladies were often wont to embroider the scarf for their knights with the figure of a bee humming around a sprig of Thyme. This two-fold symbol implied, moreover, that he who adopted it, was gentle in all his acts.

TOOTHWORT (*Lathræa squamaria*).—CONCEALMENT.

THIS plant grows only in the most hidden recesses of the grove, at the foot of large trees, in moist and shady places. Its flowers are nearly always concealed under moss or dry leaves.

THE TREMBLING POPLAR.—MOANING.

THIS beautiful tree which, in the calmest weather, produces by its rustling leaves a sound resembling that of a murmuring brook, seems to moan under the influence of the lightest wind. It would appear to harmonize with the touching notes of the nightingale, when she bewails the loss of her young, as noticed by Virgil :

" So mourning 'neath the trembling poplar's shade
  The nightingale bemoans her absent young,
  Which some hard-hearted rustic, noting well,
  Drew from their nest, unplumed : now she, distressed,
  Weeps through the night, and, perching on a branch,
  Repeats her mournful song ; and with sad plaints
  Fills up the grove extended far and wide."—
                                    Favourite Field Flowers.

TREMBLING GRASS (*Briza media*).—FRIVOLITY.

FRENCH shepherds call this plant, *Amourette*, perhaps
because of its pleasant and varied appearance. They look
upon it as the emblem of a slight and transient attachment ;
for a lover is suspected of insincerity if he presents his
inamorato with a bouquet bound together with this grass. It
is, however, one of the prettiest of our grasses, and a bunch of
them in a vase is a most pleasing ornament.

TREMELLA.—RESISTANCE. OPPOSITION.

THIS is a gelatinous plant, which has engaged the attention
of the learned, but has hitherto withstood all their researches.
It was celebrated among alchemists, who made use of it in
preparing the philosopher's stone and the universal panacea ;
regarding it as an emanation from the stars. Some have
supposed these gelatinous substances to be the ejected pellets
of herons after feeding on frogs ; others have regarded it as
an animal. It seems to have transformed itself into many
analogous plants, as if determined to elude the inquiries of

the curious. It is found in garden paths and meadows. In truth we have no positive knowledge of the Tremella. It is a secret of Nature which is as little to be understood as the " everybody says so" of the unlettered mind.

TULIP (*Tulipa sylvestris*).—DECLARATION OF LOVE.

ON the banks of the Bosphorus, the Tulip represents Inconstancy; but it also is the emblem of the most violent love. Those which grow naturally in the fields of Byzantium, with petals of fiery red and centres black as though burnt, say to a captive beauty, that one loves her, and, if she will show herself to him for a moment, her appearance will make his countenance as of fire, and his heart like coal. Thus a young man fresh or *green* from the hands of nature, yields an homage without disguise ; but when fashioned by the world, as the tulip is manipulated by the hands of the gardener, he becomes more amiable, more lovely, but he has ceased to love.

The Tulip is so called from its shape resembling that of the turban. Its emblematic power, if it does not sufficiently express a declaration of love, may well speak of that mania which exceeded the madness of the most ardent lover in times past ; for under its influence men did the most insane things. Poets have written in raptures of it. Hear Thomson,

> " Then comes the Tulip race, where beauty play
> Her idle freaks. From family diffused
> To family, as flies the father dust,

201

> The varied colours run ; and while they break
> On the charmed eye, th' exulting florist marks
> With secret pride, the wonders of his hand."

and then Kleist asks,

> " Who thus, O Tulip ! thy gay painted breast,
> In all the colours of the sun hath drest !
> Well could I call thee, in thy gaudy pride,
> The queen of flowers ;"

but alas ! it has not her fragrance ; rather we may say of it,

> " Yet no delicious scent it yields, to cheer the garden or the fields,
> Vainly in gaudy colours drest, 'tis rather gazed on than caressed."

VENUS'S LOOKING-GLASS (*Campanula Speculum*).—
FLATTERY.

THIS is a pretty annual border-flower of great beauty, which, from May to August, opens its shining purple flowers in our fields so soon as the sun sheds his golden light upon them. If clouds should intercept his rays, then the sensitive petals close themselves as at the approach of night. A fanciful fable tells us that Venus let one of her mirrors fall upon the earth. A shepherd found this *bijou*, and looking upon it, as it had the power of reflecting an image more beautiful than the reality, he forgot his mistress, and cared for nothing but to admire himself in the glass. Cupid, fearing the consequences of so great an error, broke the glass and transformed the pieces into this pretty Campanula, which has ever since borne the name of Venus's Looking-glass.

VERVAIN (*Verbena officinalis*).—ENCHANTMENT.

VERVAIN was made use of by the ancients in different kinds of divination. A thousand various properties were assigned to it, among others the power of reconciling enemies. Whenever the Romans had occasion to send heralds to other nations, with a message of peace or war, one of them wore a wreath of vervain. To this custom our native poet Dryden alludes,

> " A wreath of Vervain heralds wear, amongst our garlands named,
> Being sent that dreadful news to bear, offensive war proclaimed."

The Druids held this plant in high esteem, and did not venture to gather it until they had offered sacrifice to the Earth; and now, in the north of France, the shepherds are said to collect this sacred plant with ceremonies and words known only to themselves. Thus in our time, as in the days of the ancients, Vervain is looked upon as the emblem of Enchantment.

THE VINE (*Vitis vinifera*).—INTOXICATION.

ANACHARSIS used to say that the Vine bore three kinds of fruit,—intoxication, voluptuousness, and repentance; and that he who was temperate in his speech, moderate in his diet, and innocent in his amusements, was a perfect man.

The Vine, notwithstanding that its produce has been, and

is still, greatly abused, is one of the most valuable gifts of nature. Its fruit, when ripe and fresh from the tree, is most delicious and refreshing; when dried it adds to our enjoyment of the food given to us, and is a most wholesome part of our diet; and in the form of wine expressed from the grape, it is not only innocuous but invigorating when used within proper limits. The effects in no case should exceed what we call mirthfulness; as Scott says,

> " Let dimpled mirth his temples twine,
> With tendrils of the laughing Vine ;"

and if it do more than "gladden the heart of man, and make him of a cheerful countenance," it produces results which invariably follow upon the abuse of those good things which have been given to us ; for every created thing is good, and to be rightly received with thankful heart.

WHITE WATER LILY (*Nymphæa alba*).—ELOQUENCE.

THE Egyptians consecrated the Nymphæa Lotus to the Sun, the god of Eloquence. These flowers close at sunset and sink into the water ; they rise with the god of day as he comes above the horizon. The flower forms part of the head-dress of Osiris. Indian gods are depicted sitting on a Lotus-flower at the bottom of the waters; symbolizing, as it would seem, the rising up of the Earth, and its separation from the Water.

Our White Water Lily is a lovely sister of the Egyptian Lotus. Well may Miss Twamley give the invitation,

> " Oh ! come to the river's rim, come to us there,
>   For the White Water Lily is wondrous fair ;"

and much more she sweetly sings of its praises in her
" Romance of Flowers."

THE WALL-FLOWER (*Cheiranthus fruticulosus*).— FAITHFUL IN ADVERSITY.

" Recesses where the Wall-flower grew."—SCOTT.

WE find this fragrant flower blooming in places where ruin
and desolation prevail. In the cracks of ancient walls, in
nooks and corners of shattered towers, on cottages and tombs
in decay, there we may find the wall-flower, in short, wherever
adversity and misfortune have befallen masonry of old, valued
for what it has been, there this flower flourishes, faithful to
the friends who cherished it when they were prosperous and
gay. Thus Delta (Moir) has sung of it,

> " The Wall-flower—the Wall-flower, how beautiful it blooms !
>   It gleams above the ruined tower, like sunlight over tombs ;
>   It sheds a halo of repose around the wrecks of time ;—
>   To beauty give the flaunting rose, the Wall-flower is sublime.
>
>   Flower of the solitary place ! grey ruin's golden crown !
>   Thou lendest melancholy grace to haunts of old renown;
>   Thou mantlest o'er the battlement, by strife or storm decayed ;
>   And fillest up each envious rent Time's canker-tooth hath made."

THE WEEPING WILLOW (*Salix babylonica*).— MELANCHOLY.

THIS noble tree never meets our eye, but we call to mind the melancholy, but beautiful words of the sacred poet, " By the waters of Babylon we sat down and wept, when we remembered thee, O Sion ! As for our harps, we hanged them up, upon the willows that are therein." Thus mournfully bewailing their beloved Sion, whence they had been led captive, beneath the pendulous branches of this graceful tree, they have caused it ever since to be regarded as the emblem of Melancholy. Bidlake looks upon it as ever sorrowful :

> " The Willow tribes that ever weep,
> Hang drooping o'er the glassy-bosomed wave."

The association of melancholy feelings with the Willow of Babylon, seems to be communicated to others of the tribe. We well remember the saddening, but pleasing influence which a long row of silver-leaved Willows, growing on the grassy bank of the silvery Dearne, in Yorkshire, had upon us. Often did we, in our boyish days, stand or recline under their shade, in the glowing heat of summer, and, looking on the water, feel refreshed. There, too, in sweet interchange of thought with one who has long since entered into his rest, we conversed, ever and anon quoting passages from favourite poets, whose words seemed to ring out with a peculiar charm and freshness in that pleasant spot.

Among the many interesting specimens of this tree is one

in the churchyard of West Harptre, Somersetshire, said to have been brought from St. Helena, where Napoleon, from 1815 to 1822, had leisure to review his nineteen years of life, spent amid scenes of carnage and bloodshed, and to mourn over the schemes of ambition, which he had planned and striven to carry out, frustrated and annihilated. This now magnificent tree is stated to have been planted by the Rev. G. T. Hudson, vicar, 1837-42.

WHEAT.—RICHES.

"Now waving grain, wide o'er the plain,
Delights the weary farmer,"—BURNS.

WHEN he, seated upon a rustic stile, looks down, right and left, upon the valleys beneath, standing so thick with corn, that they seem to laugh and sing; and thither we would gladly wend our way to share his pleasure, as if in answer to Miss Twamley's summons,

"Come, let us rest on yon rude stile where stand
The village children, and look o'er the sea
Of golden-coloured grain, that waves beneath
The gentle breath of the soft Summer's day."

Meet emblem of Riches is the golden wheat, for is it not to the children of men the most important element of that annual shower of wealth which falls, as it were, direct from heaven, to feed and sustain in life, not only the human race, but every living thing that hath breath! And the abundance, and excellence of quality, of the Wheat of this present year, 1868, are such as has scarcely ever been known, and may not be again seen for many, many years to come.

WHITE HEATHER.—Good Luck.

Extract from our beloved Queen's Book :—" Our dear Victoria (the Princess Royal) was engaged to Prince Frederick William of Prussia. He had spoken to us of his wishes; but we were uncertain whether he himself should speak to her or wait till he came back again. During our ride up *Craig-na-Ban*, he picked a piece of White Heather, the emblem of " Good Luck," which he gave to her ; this enabled him to make an allusion to his hopes and wishes, as they rode down *Glen Girnock*, which led to their happy [betrothal]."—Sept. 29, 1855.

WHITE JASMINE (*Jasminum officinale*).—Amiability.

" Luxuriant above all
The Jasmine, throwing wide her elegant sweets,
The deep dark green of whose unvarnished leaf
Makes more conspicuous, and illumines more
The bright profusion of her scattered stars."—Cowper.

There are those individuals who are endowed with such a happy temperament, that they seem thrown into the world to hold society together. They have in their manners so much complaisance and grace, that they well sustain every

Moss Rose — Sweet Scented Violet — White Jasmine

position into which they are cast. They accommodate themselves to the taste, and properly estimate the mind, of all
others. They are so obliging, that they always interest
themselves in what you say to them ; they are oblivious of
themselves to serve you, and they are silent to listen to you.
They flatter no one, assume nothing, never give offence.
Their character is a heavenly gift, like that of personal
charms. They please, in short, because Nature has made
them amiable.

Of this characteristic Amiability the Jasmine has long been
considered a most appropriate emblem.

WHITE LILAC.—Youth.

On account of the purity and brief duration of its beautiful
thyrses, the White Lilac is the emblem of Youth, that fleet
and charming period of life which all the treasures of the
world are unable to restore.

WHITE MULBERRY (*Morus alba*).—Wisdom.

The White Mulberry has ever been called the wisest of
trees, because it is very slow in developing its leaves. There
is a saying, "Foolish as the Almond Tree, wise as the
Mulberry," because the Almond is always the first to bloom.
A sprig of the Almond Tree together with a sprig of the
White Mulberry, say, Wisdom should be joined with Activity.

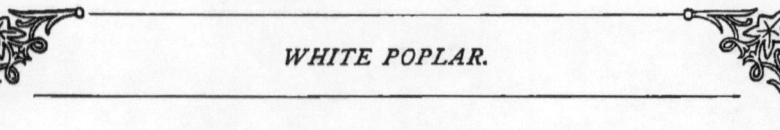

WHITE POPLAR (*Populus alba*).—TIME.

THIS tree grows to eighty feet high, with a magnificent head upon a straight stem, covered with a silver bark. The ancients dedicated it to Time, because the leaves of this beautiful tree are in continual agitation, and, being brown on one side and white on the other, represent the alternation of day and night.

WHITE POPPY.—SLEEP OF THE HEART,

BECAUSE the tasteless oil expressed from Poppy seeds calms the nerves and induces sleep.

WHITE ROSE.—SILENCE.

" O goddess, thou art wondrous queer !
When none invoke thee, then most near ;"

WROTE an old friend in a sonnet addressed to this mythological being. The deity is represented as a youthful figure, half naked, holding a finger upon the mouth, and a White Rose in the other hand. A White Rose used to be sculptured over the door of banqueting rooms, to remind the guests that they must never repeat abroad what was said in their festive moments.

WHITE VIOLET.—Candour.

Candour takes precedence, in order of time, of Modesty. The White Violet is as if the purple one were invested with the robe of innocence.

THE WHORTLE OR BILBERRY (*Vaccinium myrtillus*).— Treachery.

" Nor lacked, for more delight on that warm day,
Our table, small parade of garden fruits,
And Whortle-berries from the mountain side."—
Wordsworth.

Ænomaüs, father of the lovely Hippodamia, had Myrtillus, son of Mercury, for a shield-bearer. Being proud of this, he required that all who aspired to the hand of his daughter, should enter the lists with him in the chariot race. Pelops, anxious to secure Hippodamia, promised a high reward to Myrtillus if he would take away the bolt from his master's chariot wheels. Myrtillus took the bribe: the chariot was overthrown, and Œnomaüs killed; but with his expiring breath he prayed that the traitor should be thrown into the sea. On his body being brought to the shore for that purpose, Mercury changed it into the shrub which bears his name; that shrub resembles a little Myrtle. It is the Whortleberry. It bears an abundance of purple berries, which are juicy, but somewhat insipid.

THE WILD PLUM.—INDEPENDENCE.

THE Wild Plum Tree is said to be the least tractable of our indigenous trees. It will not bear the knife, nor allow itself to be transplanted.

WILD RUE.—MANNERS OR MORALS.

SHAKSPEARE and other old authors call this, "Herb of grace." We are told that Mercury gave to Ulysses an infusion of the root of Wild Rue to carry off the effects of the draught given to him by Circe.

HELENIUM (*H. autumnale*).—TEARS.

THE flowers of this North American plant bear some resemblance to little bright yellow suns. They flourish in the Autumn with the Asters. They are fancifully said to have sprung from the tears of Helen. Other writers assert that Helenium was the name given to a plant which that frail beauty used in preparing her cosmetics.

WITHY, OR OSIER (*Salix viminalis*).—FRANKNESS.

THERE is a proverb referring to a sincere man, which says, He is frank as an Osier. It is in this sense that a French poet has used the emblem,

"Le fier et brave Montansier,
Dont le cœur est brave comme Osier."

WOOD ANEMONE (*A. nemorosa*).—FORLORNNESS.

"The Wind-flower, pale and fragile."—M. A. BROWNE.

ANEMONE was a nymph beloved of Zephyr. This aroused the jealousy of Flora, who banished her from her court, and changed her into a flower, which always blooms before the return of Spring. Zephyr has abandoned this unfortunate beauty to the caresses of Boreas, who, failing to win her love, disturbs her, makes her bloom too early, and causes her to fade quickly.

An Anemone, with the motto, *Brevis est usus*, i.e., "Her reign is short," accurately declares the fleeting nature of her beauty.

WOOD SORREL (*Oxalis acetosella*).—JOY.

THE Hallelujah Oxalis, as the French call this plant, flourishes at Easter. Every evening it closes and bends down its leaves, folds up its corollas, and allows its flowers to hang drooping. They seem to fall with the sun ; but, at dawn of day, one might fancy that they are filled with joy, for they unfold their leaves, and spread forth their flowers. On these accounts it is said by country people, that they praise God.

The Wood Sorrel is by some thought to be the true Shamrock. It is the emblem of the Irish nation, and the badge of the Order of St. Patrick. By its means that early preacher of Christianity taught the people the great doctrine of the Trinity.

As a national emblem, Moore has written of it,

> "Where'er they pass, a triple grass
> Shoots up, with dew-drops streaming,
> As softly green, as emerald seen
> Through purest crystal gleaming.
> O the Shamrock, the green, immortal Shamrock!
> Chosen Leaf of Bard and Chief,
> Old Erin's native Shamrock!"

WORMWOOD (*Artemisia Absinthium*).—ABSENCE.

LA FONTAINE has said that Absence is the greatest of evils. Absinthe, or Wormwood, is the most bitter of plants. Its name comes from the Greeks, and means *without sweetness.* Spenser makes a maiden thus bemoan the absence of her lover:

> " So I alone, now left disconsolate,
> Mourn to myself the absence of my love,
> And wandering here and there all desolate,
> Seek with my plaints to match the mournful dove."

A WREATH OF ROSES.—THE REWARD OF VIRTUE.

WE are told that S. Medard, Bishop of Noyon, who was born at Salency, of an illustrious family, offered the most touching prize that kindness ever gave to virtue. This was a simple wreath of Roses; but to obtain this, the candidates must be humble-minded, very modest, and very prudent. The Bishop's sister received the prize from his own hands A.D. 532.

A WREATH OF WHITE DAISIES.—I WILL
THINK OF IT.

IN the days of chivalry, when a lady, to speak in common parlance, "didn't know her own mind ;" that is to say, was not determined either to accept or refuse the suit of her lover, she used to wear on her brow a Wreath of White Daisies, by which she wished to say to him; I will think of it.

YARROW (*Achillea Millefolium*).—WAR.

THIS plant is said to heal all wounds caused by iron. We have it stated that Achilles made use of it to cure the wounds he had inflicted on Telephus; but other accounts say that he was cured by the rust of the spear which caused the wound.

YELLOW NARCISSUS.—DISDAIN.

DISDAINFUL persons are for the most part exacting, and have little amiability : thus of all this genus the Yellow Narcissus is the least beautiful, most devoid of fragrance, and yet it demands more care than the rest.

YELLOW ROSE.—Unfaithfulness.

Yellow is the colour which we usually assign to faults of unfaithfulness. The Yellow Rose seems the flower which properly represents those who are guilty of it. Water wearies it, the sun burns it. Constraint can alone bring this Rose, which has no fragrance, into good condition. It does not improve with care, nor yet when it enjoys freedom. When one would wish to see it at its best, we must bend its buds down to the earth, secure them in that position, and then it will flourish.

THE YEW-TREE (*Taxus baccata*).—Sadness.

"The Yew, which, in the place of sculptured stone,
Marks out the resting-place of men unknown."—
CHURCHILL.

The Yew-tree has always been considered the suitable ornament of churchyards, and so has become associated with sad recollections. It is not a favourite tree with us. Its appearance, when left to grow at will, is gloomy and heavy. We had occasion to plant trees in a churchyard, and we preferred the cheerful Lime-tree, which has grown and prospered, and added much to the light and airy aspect of the village cemetery. We were offered some Yew-trees, which we declined with thanks. Where our brothers and sisters sleep the sleep of death, there ought we to feel all the comfort that we can feel, in the hope that they enjoy a better life than this, and

216

look forward, without dread or despondency, to the time when we shall be permitted to rejoin them.

Sir Walter Scott agrees with all other poets in regarding the Yew Tree as having a sad and gloomy appearance, and as producing a corresponding feeling in the mind. In Rokeby he describes them thus—

> " But here, 'twixt rock and river grew
> A dismal grove of sable Yew,
> With whose sad tints were mingled seen
> The blighted fir's sepulchral green.
> Seemed that the trees their shadows cast,
> The earth that nourished them to blast ;
> For never knew that swarthy grove
> The verdant hue that fairies love,
> Nor wilding green, nor woodland flower,
> Arose within its baleful bower.
> The dank and sable earth receives
> Its only carpet from the leaves,
> That, from the withering branches cast,
> Bestrewed the ground with every blast."

YOKE ELM.—Ornament.

THIS beautiful tree was formerly the principal ornament of large gardens. It was used to form long verdant screens, for porticoes, obelisks, pyramids, colonnades. Father Rapin, in his poem, *Des Jardins*, wrote a fine eulogy on this tree. We may see at Versailles how well the famed Le Notre knew to introduce it into his beautiful designs.

INDEX OF SENTIMENTS.

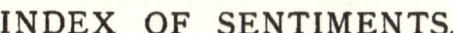

219

INDEX OF SENTIMENTS.

INDEX OF SENTIMENTS.

London: R. Clay, Sons, and Taylor, Printers.